Malcolm Braddock:
Activist. Leader. Passion...
legendary, late Congressman Braddock. Malcolm never wanted any part of Daddy Braddock's political plans for him. But little does the brooding bachelor know that a take-no-prisoners beauty has her own plans to make the number one son *her* number one mission!

Shondra Braddock:
Gorgeous. Brilliant. Wild and unstoppable. Shondra's spent her life dealing with a family of men who want to tame her. But when she embarks on a high-stakes, highly improper international affair with her sexy, *white* boss, she discovers the forbidden pleasure of being with the one man who prefers her *un*tamed....

Tyson Braddock:
Hot-tempered. Hot-bodied. And hot as hell. Workaholic Tyson put his marriage on hold for years. But he and his estranged wife are in for a seven-pound, eight-ounce surprise! Ty believes he can handle fatherhood, but can he handle the passionate new side of his suddenly not-so-predictable, but oh-so-seductive wife?

The Secret Son:
Not all of Senator Braddock's secrets died with him. Some are still very much alive, and packing a hard, six-foot-one, muscular frame to die for. But when this exotic secret son finds out his *real* identity, and ends up playing protector to a fiery virgin in the process, all bets...and clothes...are off!

Books by Adrianne Byrd

Kimani Romance

She's My Baby
When Valentines Collide
To Love a Stranger
Her Lover's Legacy

Kimani Arabesque

When You Were Mine
"Finding the Right Key" in *Takin' Chances for the Holidays*
"Wishing on a Star" in *A Season of Miracles*

ADRIANNE BYRD

has always preferred to live within the realm of her imagination, where all the men are gorgeous and the women are worth whatever trouble they manage to get into.

Her Lover's Legacy

ADRIANNE BYRD

KIMANI™
ROMANCE

If you purchased this book without a cover you should be aware
that this book is stolen property. It was reported as "unsold and
destroyed" to the publisher, and neither the author nor the
publisher has received any payment for this "stripped book."

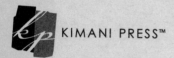

KIMANI PRESS™

ISBN-13: 978-0-373-86076-0
ISBN-10:   0-373-86076-5

HER LOVER'S LEGACY

Copyright © 2008 by Harlequin Books S.A.

All rights reserved. The reproduction, transmission or utilization
of this work in whole or in part in any form by any electronic, mechanical
or other means, now known or hereafter invented, including xerography,
photocopying and recording, or in any information storage or retrieval
system, is forbidden without written permission. For permission please
contact Kimani Press, Editorial Office, 233 Broadway, New York, NY
10279 U.S.A.

This is a work of fiction. Names, characters, places and incidents are
either the product of the author's imagination or are used fictitiously,
and any resemblance to actual persons, living or dead, business establishments,
events or locales is entirely coincidental.

® and TM are trademarks. Trademarks indicated with ® are registered in
the United States Patent and Trademark Office, the Canadian Trade Marks
Office and/or other countries.

www.kimanipress.com

Printed in U.S.A.

Dear Reader,

Welcome to Houston. I'd like to introduce you to the Braddocks, an affluent African-American family who are entrenched in secrets, sex and political intrigue. In this four-book continuity, prepare to be swept away by their powerful love stories, and discover the secret that cost this wonderful family their patriarch. I was honored to be asked to contribute to this series, and I hope you enjoy reading Malcolm and Gloria's journey to self-discovery and love.

Then run out and buy book #2, *Sex and the Single Braddock* by Robyn Amos; book #3, *Second Chance, Baby* by A.C. Arthur; and book #4, *The Object of his Protection* by Brenda Jackson.

Enjoy,

Adrianne Byrd

Chapter 1

It was the second-worst day of Malcolm Braddock's life. The first was three days ago when he received the news about his father's fatal car crash. Ever since then, he'd been walking around numb and talking in a daze.

Now, Malcolm tightened his grip around his mother's shoulders and watched the ever-graceful Evelyn Braddock draw her chin higher and somehow keep her shimmering tears from streaking down her ageless face. A forty-year marriage over without a single warning.

His baby sister, Shondra, was another story.

Though to a stranger's eye she looked calm, cool and collected, anyone who knew Shawnie wouldn't have missed the dull listlessness of her brown eyes or the dark circles that now seemed to ring them permanently, the puffy red nose rubbed raw from endless wiping. She was falling apart.

Malcolm ground his molars together, anger and helplessness finally penetrating his numb armor. Thank God for his brother, Tyson, an unexpected and welcome Rock of Gibraltar who anchored the family and kept it together.

As the eldest son, that should have been Malcolm's job.

A fine mist of rain descended from Texas's slate-gray sky while fat thunderclouds gathered menacingly above the large group of mourners surrounding Congressman Harmon Braddock's grave site. Reverend Vereen made his appeals to the heavens about mercy and forgiveness, but Malcolm had tuned all that out when the black-and-chrome casket began its descent into the freshly turned earth.

Acidic tears burned Malcolm's eyes while his breath stalled in his lungs. *No! Wait! I'm not ready yet.* But time, like it had for the past three days, refused to stop and wait for him to catch up.

His father was dead.

"In sure and in certain hope of the Resurrection to eternal life through our Lord," the Reverend intoned, "we commit Brother Harmon Braddock to the ground. Earth to earth, ashes to ashes, dust to dust…"

Malcolm closed his eyes and blocked out the rest of the Burial Rite.

When it was all over, mourners cloistered around the family, once again offering their condolences. Many, if not most, Malcolm recognized as his father's political allies, supporters and even adversaries. Their slick hands and painted-on smiles turned his stomach, but he knew it was all a part of the game—even for Houston local media outlets filming a comfortable distance away.

"Your father was a great man." Senator Ray Cayman's strong, wiry hand pressed into Malcolm's. "I know the last two years—"

"Yes. Thank you, Senator," Malcolm said in a near growl, and freed his hand from the steel grip. He knew the direction the conversation was headed and he didn't want to go there. Not now. Probably never.

If Cayman was offended, it didn't show in his weathered mahogany features. Actually, Malcolm couldn't remember a time when the distinguished septuagenarian showed his true emotions, but he knew his cool brown eyes missed nothing.

With a slight nod, Cayman stepped aside and in his place a tall African-American man with unusual Asian-shaped eyes shook his hand. "Sorry for your loss," he said with a curt nod, and then moved on.

The line of endless faces continued, and Malcolm returned to feeling more like a marble statue than a man still among the living.

Just then, Bruce Hanlon stepped up to Malcolm. "You know your father was like a brother to me," Bruce stressed. The comment almost wrestled a smile from Malcolm. Nobody would have mistaken the affluent blue-eyed judge and the rich ebony-hued Harmon Braddock as brothers, but the two had always been as thick as thieves as far back as Malcolm could remember.

"He loved you," Hanlon added, refusing to relinquish their handshake until Malcolm met his sharp gaze. "You know that, don't you?"

Did he? Malcolm pressed his lips together and gave the judge a firm nod. It was the best he could do.

A familiar melodious voice floated on the air. "Please let me know if there's anything I can do."

He caught sight of his father's assistant, Gloria Kingsley, talking to his brother, Ty, and his wife, Felicia. Malcolm's chest tightened as he watched Gloria's beautiful golden eyes turn toward Shawnie, her arms wrapping around his sister in shared comfort.

He hadn't meant to stare while the women held each other, but when Gloria's gaze caught his, he turned away.

Thunder rolled and a flash of lightning streaked the evening sky. It was a welcome excuse to usher his mother to their waiting limousine before the light drizzle turned into a torrential downpour and before he had to face Gloria on his own.

Hours later, the day finally came to an exhausting end with Malcolm peeling out of his suit before he finished entering his quaint inner-city apartment. He had tossed the jacket over the back of the sofa, removed his shoes near the breakfast bar and unbuttoned his shirt by the time he retrieved a Sam Adams from the refrigerator. The pull from his beer was a balm to his tattered nerves. The second chug emptied the bottle, and he had to grab another before returning to the spacious living room.

He collapsed on the Italian leather sofa and stared up at the strange flower patterns in the ceiling, trying his damnedest to clear his mind and hang on to the protective numbness that surrounded his heart.

It wasn't working.

Images of that heated fight he and his father had two years ago flashed before his eyes. There was so much he regretted, so many words he didn't mean.

That's a lie, his conscience corrected. He *had* meant them at the time.

"You used to be a man of integrity—a man of his word. Now you're like every other slick politician in Washington. You're one of them—a sellout!"

Malcolm closed his eyes, trying unsuccessfully to block out the image of his father's angry face, slack and drained of color as he'd shouted those words and stormed out of his father's office. In his escape, he'd nearly bowled over a shocked Gloria.

True, in his thirty-two years he and his father had butt heads in the past, but not like that. Never like that.

When Malcolm was growing up, Harmon Braddock was his hero. He was the top prosecutor in the district attorney's office, putting away bad guys and throwing away the key. It was the closest thing to an Eliot Ness that he and his friends knew. Of course, Malcolm would embellish the stories a bit whenever a member of some crime cartel was sent to jail, but it was always in good childhood fun.

When his father accepted the position as head legal council for Senator Ray Cayman, Malcolm's interest marched in line with his father's and he entered Morehouse for a double major in political science and history.

Years later, there were no words to describe how happy and proud he felt when his father not only decided to run, but won his seat in the House of Representatives.

Sometime during the end of his stint at Morehouse College, Malcolm began championing some of his mother's philanthropic causes: Feed the Hungry, UNICEF and the Coalition for the Homeless—the list went on and on. When it was time for Malcolm to ship out to Harvard Law, he'd really connected with his mother's work and had serious doubts whether politics was the right course for his life.

He brought the question up to his father, and it was perhaps the first time his father showed a flicker of disappointment in him. Feeling as if he'd somehow betrayed his father, Malcolm still entered and aced law school. But the hypocrisy of the political landscape sickened him even more.

Once he'd passed the bar, he shunned all the lofty positions offered to one whose father was a star congressman. Instead, he joined the Peace Corps and hopped the first plane smoking out of the United States.

For four years, Malcolm toiled happily in Ghana, strengthening and teaching behavior changes to reduce water- and sanitation-related diseases.

Unfortunately, his extended absence had cost him his first serious relationship with Theresa

Frost, his college girlfriend who'd once promised to wait for him. Instead, when he returned, she had moved to New York and married some rich studio executive.

He was crushed.

His father thought once he'd returned to Houston that he'd worked out all his philanthropic demons and would now utilize his law degree and accept a position with the D.A.'s office, which would eventually lead to a life in politics. Instead, Malcolm founded the Arc Foundation—which in four years he had transformed into one of the world's largest grassroots organizations of and for people with intellectual and developmental disabilities.

The tug-of-war between what Malcolm wanted and what his father wanted for him had just begun.

And now it's over. You're free.

Malcolm sat up, ashamed of the renegade thought. However, the guilt refused to go away. Instead, it clung to him like a living thing, choking him.

Hitting the shower, he scrubbed his skin as the steaming water pelted down. The pain distracted him.

Somewhat refreshed, Malcolm returned to the living room and scanned the sparsely decorated apartment with its few family pictures. *Ah, here it is.* A broken wood-framed five-by-eight picture of his father with the glass splintered like a spider's web. It had been shoved in the bottom of a box inside the DVD cabinet.

It was his father's official press kit photo, one with him dressed in an immaculate dark suit, perched behind a handsome mahogany desk with an American flag on his lapel and full-size flag propped in the corner.

Congressman Harmon Braddock, a man for the people.

Yeah, the rich people.

Malcolm lowered the picture back into the box and shifted his attention to a few DVDs labeled Dad's Campaign. He had no intentions of doing it, had no idea whether he was ready for it, but he opened the DVD case and slipped the first disk into the player and clicked on the TV.

Images of the first Braddock's Victory Campaign Party splashed onto the screen. Malcolm and the entire family stood proudly behind his father, waving through falling streamers, balloons and confetti to a jubilant crowd holding flags, signs and bumper stickers in the air.

The corners of Malcolm's mouth curved, the memories of that wonderful night warming his body. When the camera zoomed in on his father's face, he pressed Pause on the remote control and then studied the face that was so similar to his own:

open, honest and *intelligent* were adjectives everyone used to describe Harmon Braddock.

At least in the beginning.

Malcolm rolled his eyes at the voice inside his head that was determined to play devil's advocate and unfroze the frame. But seconds later, he paused the picture again. This time the image filling his forty-eight-inch screen was of Gloria Kingsley.

He was surprised to see her—an unexpected beaming face in the crowd. He hadn't known that she was there that night. Gloria hadn't started working for his father until toward the end of his second term in D.C.

She couldn't have been more than—what?—twenty-one. Of course, he had no idea how old the golden-eyed beauty was; it was certainly not something a man asked a woman, either. If he had to guess, he'd say she was twenty-nine. One thing was clear, Gloria Kingsley was pretty when she was younger, but she was nothing less than a knockout now.

A pain-in-the-ass knockout, but a knockout all the same.

The first time he'd met the woman was during a rare political fund-raiser his father talked him into attending. Gloria entered the ballroom in an unforgettable black, backless evening gown that had every man with a pulse tripping over his tongue.

Malcolm raced to her side, swiping an extra flute of champagne in his haste. When he offered her the champagne, she shot him down by telling him she didn't drink, that his tie was crooked, and then inquired when was the last time his suit had seen the inside of a cleaners. From then on out, Malcolm didn't like her.

Of course, she absolutely mooned over his father and could regurgitate ad nauseam every speech, point of view and interview the man had ever made.

Malcolm made it a point to stay away from her.

Still, he thought she was a gorgeous woman.

The doorbell rang, and Malcolm groaned his irritation and considered not answering the door, but by the time his uninvited guest rang the bell a fourth time, he hopped up and stormed toward it. When he snatched it open, his vast vocabulary failed to suggest a single word for his unexpected, albeit beautiful, guest: Gloria.

Chapter 2

Momentarily thrown off guard by the sight of the smooth, muscular, toffee-colored skin peeking from the open V of Malcolm's burgundy robe, Gloria unconsciously licked her lips and fluttered a hand to her throat. "Did I catch you at a bad time?"

Malcolm's groomed brows crashed together above his probing brown eyes a second before his rumbling baritone snapped impatiently, "What are you doing here?"

Stung by the rebuff, Gloria squared her shoulders and wielded a sharp look of her own. "Well, I certainly didn't come here to stand out in the hallway."

They stared at each other, locked in a stalemate.

Gloria had feared this would happen, especially judging how Malcolm went out of his way to avoid her at the funeral, but she had also resolved to camp outside his door if that's what it took to get him to see reason.

Finally, Malcolm stepped back and allowed her to enter through a narrowed space. Refusing to be intimidated, she crossed the threshold. Her breasts brushed against what felt to her like molten steel; volts of electricity surged through her body. She jumped.

"Must be static from the carpet," Malcolm explained, confirming he'd felt the charge as well.

She moved on, glanced around and was impressed by the simple decor and surprising cleanliness of a confirmed-bachelor's pad. When she entered the living room, she froze and stared at her own image on the television screen.

Malcolm scrambled from behind her, grabbed the remote from the couch and punched the power button. Once the screen went black, the room roared with a strained and uncomfortable silence. "I, uh, was looking at some old campaign stuff and, uh, well, paused it when you knocked."

"I see," she said.

He tossed the remote back on the couch and faced her. "Okay. So you're not standing in the hallway," he said, reclaiming his previous impatience. "What is it that you want?"

Why Gloria's gaze tumbled from his penetrating coffee-brown eyes to his deliciously plump lips at the question was beyond her. As to why her stomach looped into knots whenever she was around him? She didn't even want to go there.

"First," she began, and then cleared her throat from what felt like a sack of marbles clogging her windpipe. "I wanted to extend my condolences for your terrible loss, Malcolm."

When he gave her a small, almost imperceptible nod, she trudged on. "I know the past two years—"

"Stop." Despite the soft tone, the order held the authority of a military commander. "I appreciate your coming here and all, but, uh, if you came looking for an Oprah moment, I'm afraid I'm going to have to disappoint you."

Slowly, Gloria tilted her head side to side and cracked the bones in her neck while she prayed for patience. What was it about Malcolm that got under her skin? From the first time they met, the sarcastic know-it-all rubbed her the wrong way.

Why had she thought tonight would be any different?

"Anything else?" he prompted.

His abhorrent rudeness forced Gloria to silently

count to ten. However, Malcolm took her silence as confirmation that she was through. He grasped her by the elbow to direct her back to the front door.

The touch of his hand shot off a few more sparks, but Gloria planted her feet and jerked her arm free. "I'm not finished yet!"

Malcolm sighed, rolled his eyes and shoved his hands into his pockets, widening the V of his robe and displaying a larger swath of honey-brown skin.

Gloria licked her lips again.

"Well?" he said, staring. "I'm sure you understand I've had a very long day."

"I need you," she said. When his brows crashed together again, she realized what she'd said hadn't come out right. "I meant, I need you to come to Harmon's—I mean, your father's—office and help pack up his things."

He was laughing before she finished the sentence.

"Malcolm—"

"Sorry," he said, still chuckling and shaking his head. "You've come to the wrong one. This is a job for Shawnie or Ty or maybe even Mom."

"Don't be ridiculous," she scolded. "You're the oldest—the head of the family. This is *your* job."

He went from laughing to scowling in less than two seconds. "I don't need you to tell me what my job is, Ms. Kingsley."

"Oh, really?" Gloria arched her brows and crossed her arms. "You think it was your job to hole up in this apartment for the past three days and watch old videos instead of being at your mother's and helping the rest of your family through this difficult time?"

He said nothing, but Gloria saw a vein appear and twitch along his jawline.

Still, she continued. "The way I see things, the *least* you could do is help me with Harmon's office."

"The problem with the way you see things, Ms. Kingsley, is that nobody cares—especially me."

His words were a verbal slap, but she reeled back as if it was physical. Her chin came up, but when her tears came unbidden, she barely held them in check. "If it makes you feel better to lash out at me, then please by all means, do so. You're hurting, and I understand it devastates the male ego to show any type of vulnerability—especially around a woman. But when you're finished attacking me for your personal issues, I *still* need for you to help pack your father's belongings."

They stood in a stalemate.

"It shouldn't take too long," she added, gentler this time. "Plus, there's a lot of legal stuff that you would have a better handle on than I would. And it might be one last thing you can do for him."

Malcolm drew a deep breath. The protruding vein disappeared, and for one brief moment, Gloria thought she saw his eyes soften. Had she hit the nail on the head?

"Two hours—tops," she lied.

After a long silence, Malcolm nodded and surprised her. "Sorry. What I said was…I'm sorry."

"Apology accepted." Gloria relaxed enough to smile. "Truce?"

A corner of his mouth twitched. "Truce." He opened his arms and she automatically stepped into his embrace. Arms like steel bands wrapped and pressed her against an equally hard body. His skin smelled fresh, like soap.

Gloria closed her eyes and drew strength and comfort from a man she'd often found herself at odds with—and she took it. Greedily.

She must have lost track of time because she jumped when Malcolm cleared his throat. She had to extract herself from his warm embrace, so they endured yet another awkward moment.

"So, um, Monday?" she asked.

"Monday it is," he confirmed with a studying gaze.

She cleared her throat and straightened her posture. It was time to make her exit. She'd got what she came for: the first step of many in her master plan.

Chapter 3

Malcolm needed to get his head examined.

His father's office was the last place he wanted to be, and after that strange visit from Gloria a couple of days ago, he wasn't too sure if it was a smart idea to be alone with her in any capacity. If he hadn't gotten her to release him when he did, Gloria Kingsley would have felt something else rising from beneath his robe.

Actually, he was sort of curious how she would've reacted. Heaven knows it was a surprise to him, but the combination of her floral-scented perfume and her soft curves pressed against him awakened something within.

Something he didn't want to explore.

Now staring up at the brick-and-glass building of his father's local office, Malcolm scanned his mental Rolodex of excuses for one that would get him out of going inside.

Something other than the fact that he simply didn't want to do this. He wasn't ready. He may never be ready.

He sat in his car, watching a few employees trickle out, carrying their boxes of belongings— each unemployed now that Harmon Braddock had passed away.

The brave soul who would run for the vacant Twenty-ninth Congressional District seat would hire his own professional crew, but a few, like Gloria, would remain and help with whatever transition was needed from the old guard to the new.

Then what will she do? Malcolm wondered.

The question puzzled him, and he had to admit he really didn't know that much about Gloria's personal life or her history. He just knew the meticulously organized woman who ran his father's office like a well-oiled machine. As far as he knew, she was never late, always professional and thought the sun rose and set on Harmon Braddock.

Simply put, her hero worship of his father annoyed him.

But say what he will, his father seemed equally impressed and dependent on Gloria as well—to the point that she was like a second daughter, a feeling that seemed mutually expressed by Malcolm's mother as well.

Shawnie and Tyson were also cast under her spell and had bragged about her on more than one occasion. Yep, everyone loved Gloria, and yet whenever she and Malcolm were in the same room atoms and neutrons collided.

"C'mon. Let's get this over with." He removed the keys from the ignition and climbed out of his silver hybrid SUV. "Whatever you do, stay calm. Don't let her bait you or get under your skin," he coached, as if he was gearing up for his old college football games.

"Malcolm." A familiar voice whipped out at him as he lumbered up the sidewalk. He looked up and smiled into Mrs. Blake's kind face. Something about the grandmotherly southern woman made him think of Little League and homemade apple pies. Nothing about her said politics, but in truth she was one impressive campaign manager.

"Hello, Mrs. Blake," he greeted her when he reached her. He stooped over and kissed each side of her face and enjoyed the sound of her lighthearted giggles.

"Such a handsome boy," she murmured, like she always did when their paths crossed. "What a lovely service your family put together this past weekend. Your father was a very special man." Her eyes shimmered. "I can't tell you how much he'll be missed."

"We'll all miss him," he said, combating his own tears.

"You know, I don't even understand why he was driving himself that night," she said. "He usually had his personal driver, Joe, take him everywhere."

Malcolm nodded solemnly. "I guess he just felt like driving himself that night," he said. "The police report said he had to be speeding when he lost control of the car and skidded off the road. The car flipped over and…"

"Don't do this to yourself. You know he was so proud of you." Mrs. Blake gave his right cheek a loving pat. "I know the past two years…"

Malcolm tensed and dropped his gaze.

Mrs. Blake patiently tilted up his chin; her smile never wavered. "He loved you," she said succinctly.

"I know," he answered, and received another pat on the cheek.

They quickly said their goodbyes and Malcolm trudged the rest of the way to his father's old stomping ground. The moment he entered through the doors, the few people remaining all turned in their chairs. Most of them smiled, while the others gave sympathetic shakes of their heads.

He gave everyone an awkward wave.

"There you are, Malcolm," Gloria said, rounding the corner and rescuing him before the curious descended.

"I didn't know so many people were still going to be here," he whispered, trailing behind her military-like march to his father's office.

"There's still a lot of work that needs to be done," she said simply. "A lot of loose ends."

He nodded and made a quick glance at his watch. Two hours, he reminded himself.

"I saw you sitting in your car," she went on. "I was beginning to think you were going to chicken out."

Malcolm's back stiffened. "It feels a bit too soon to be doing this," he defended.

"And yet it still needs to be done," she said, rejecting the excuse.

He huffed under his breath, thinking she was more robot than woman.

Gloria walked over to the far right side of the office where a mahogany bookshelf held a library of his father's law books. "This was Harmon's personal collection. I believe it was passed down from your grandfather. I have these containers," she pointed to a stack of blue Wal-Mart brand plastic

tubs. "They are labeled and ready. Over here…"
She pointed to another bookshelf. "As you can see,
these are filled with Harmon's personal pictures,
awards and other personal effects. Those can go
into these labeled clear tubs. I sent Mabel out to find
us some bubble wrap and foam popcorn so we can
minimize potential damages."

For that, he did roll his eyes. "I don't think all that
was necessary."

"Don't be silly. Of course it was necessary," she
said, and then flittered to another section of the
office, where she had more containers labeled. Soon
he tuned out her endless prattle and wondered when
they were actually going to get down to the business
of packing boxes. When she reached the file
cabinets and started in on personal tax records
versus business travel expenses, Malcolm concluded this was definitely going to take more than
a couple of hours.

Amazingly, she didn't stop there. There was stuff
on the desk, in the desk, pictures on the walls,
pictures on the shelves. It was all mind-numbingly
dull. Which was the *only* reason Malcolm's gaze
drifted to study Gloria's petite body sheathed in a
tight, gray pencil skirt (as Shawnie called them)
and a cloud-white blouse that perhaps had one
button too many open.

Every once in a while when Gloria dipped or turned, he would get a peek of a creamy-brown breast or a black lace bra. It was a cheap thrill, but he was more than willing to take it…and enjoy it.

"Maybe I should get us some coffee before we get started," Gloria suggested, turning and almost catching him staring.

She waited a moment, and then he realized that he was supposed to say something. "I'm sorry. What was that?"

"Coffee?" she asked, folding her arms and pulling her shirt open a bit and exposing a fair amount of what he guessed was a C-cup.

She was still waiting.

He caught and cleared his throat. "Yeah, um, coffee would be great."

Gloria nodded and placed the clipboard Malcolm hadn't noticed she held down on his father's old desk. "How would you like that? Cream, sugar?"

"Black…if you don't mind."

Her full lips split into an instant smile. "Just like your father."

A frustrated sigh escaped his chest before he thought better to contain his irritation.

"I'll be right back," she said, unfazed or ignoring the response. "You can go ahead and get started," she tossed over her shoulder as she headed toward the door.

Malcolm's gaze traveled down her, taking in her every curve until she slipped out of the door. He sighed and then shook his head clear of the direction his thoughts were heading. He turned around and crashed gazes with his father's portrait hanging on the wall.

"What?" he mumbled toward his father's stern expression. "Can't a man look?"

Drawing a deep breath, Malcolm turned and walked to one of the sturdy mahogany shelves lined with photographs. As his eyes brushed across a collage of images that summed up his father's life, tears rose unrelentingly.

Family pictures were mixed with his father posing with the president of the United States, the vice president, the speaker of the House and even his father's good friends, Senator Cayman and Judge Hanlon.

Harmon Braddock in his element.

Was it a life well lived? Had his father accomplished everything he'd set out to do? Was his father happy about the man he'd become?

Malcolm drew in a deep breath, wondering if he would ever know the answer to any of those questions. His father certainly wasn't the man he'd once idolized.

Selecting one iron-and-glass frame, he studied the photograph he'd known most of his life: the picture of his father and mother on their wedding day. His mother, an extraordinary beauty for any era, clung to and smiled up at her new husband through love-filled eyes. It was as if his mother knew without a doubt she'd married her second half, her heart, her soul mate.

Harmon Braddock held his wife with equal fervor; his promise to love and cherish was evident in his expression. Everyone who'd ever seen this photograph commented on how striking and in love the couple seemed.

To which his father always replied, "How can one not fall in love with Evelyn?"

Malcolm smiled at the sound of his father's voice echoing from a distant memory while his gaze caressed the picture. He'd always loved this picture, for reasons more clear to him now than ever before. His parents' love was a rarity. Nowadays, marriages didn't last as long nor did they seem to strengthen over time. As much as their love was inspiring, though, it was also intimidating.

How did one *know* without any doubts they'd met their destiny? Malcolm thought he'd met her once but he'd been wrong.

Setting the photo down, he casually glanced at

another. Shawnie receiving her law degree from the University of Texas, Ty and Felicia's official engagement photo…

"Okay," Gloria said, breezing back into the office with two steaming cups. "Black coffee for you and one hot tea for me."

Whatever heartache Malcolm experienced was temporarily forgotten when he faced Gloria and noticed in her approach a fuller display of her creamy brown breasts thrust high in a black-laced bra.

"Here you go," she said, trying to extend the mug out to him a second time.

He lifted his hand but his mouth had slackened.

She frowned and then followed his line of vision to see another button had worked its way free.

"Oh, my God!" She thrust the cup toward him; his coffee sloshed over the rim and burned them both.

Malcolm winced but managed to hold on to the cup.

Gloria jerked her hand back, waved it in the air as she turned toward the large desk and set her tea down in order to attend to the blouse. "You know you could have said something," she snapped.

"Sorry," he said with little conviction. "I was working on it."

"Yeah. Right."

Lips curving, Malcolm rather liked seeing

Gloria's feathers ruffled, especially since before now he didn't think such a thing was possible. "Look, Gloria. I—"

"Forget it," she muttered while glancing around the floor. "Just help me find the button."

Still wearing a smile, Malcolm launched into an immediate investigation for the missing clear button against the office's champagne-colored carpet. That is, until Gloria lowered herself onto all fours and drew Malcolm's attention to her glorious apple bottom.

"It has to be around here somewhere," Gloria mumbled, fanning her hands across the carpet as she crawled her way back toward the door.

Time seemed to stop as Malcolm watched Gloria inch her way up the carpet. A near-unbearable heat scorched up the column of his neck and burned the tips of his ears. Malcolm fingered his collar loose, mistakenly thinking that it was the cause of his inability to get air into his lungs. Not to mention the unexpected throb and ache against his pants' inseam.

Just the sight of the uptight and always-proper assistant kneeling down on all fours made him fantasize about what else that position was good for.

"Here it is. I found it," Gloria exclaimed, pushing up to sit on her haunches.

Malcolm came out of his trance quick enough to set his coffee down and offer his hand to help her up. "Glad that crisis is over with," he joked, but his throat was still clogged with the residue of lust.

When Gloria arched a delicately groomed brow, he quickly coughed as a lame cover.

"Thanks," she said, placing her hand into his.

At the feel of her silky palm sliding into his, Malcolm was sure his body temperature soared into the triple digits.

What the hell was wrong with him? He couldn't stand Ms. Gloria "Know-It-All" Kingsley.

Right?

Just then, as if to rescue them from themselves, Mabel burst into the office with her arms bursting with packing material.

"I got everything you asked for, Gloria," she said, finding a nice clear spot in the center of the room and dropping everything. "Whew!" She straightened her back just as her eyes widened to twice their size. "Malcolm," she exclaimed, rushing around the pile of packing material and then pulling him into her pillow-soft body.

If Mabel was ever to enter into a celebrity look-alike contest, she would win for Star Jones (presurgery) hands down. "Gloria said that you were coming in here to help pack this stuff, but I kept telling her that it was just too soon for you to be dealing with all this right now."

Malcolm shot a glance at Gloria, triumphant that someone agreed with him.

A frown settled around the corners of Gloria's lips.

"It's still work that needs to be done," he said, quoting the efficient assistant and managing to bring a smile back to her face.

"I think we'd better get started," she said.

Malcolm readily agreed. "Will you be joining us, Mabel?"

"Unfortunately not. I have four hungry teenage boys and a construction-worker husband who'd be rumbling up a storm if dinner isn't on the table on time. But I'll be seeing you again soon, I hope."

He smiled. "You can count on it."

"Good. Good." Mabel turned toward Gloria and her smile dropped. "Ms. Kingsley," she hissed, and then covered a hand over her own bosom. "Your blouse."

"Oh, yes." Gloria blinked. "I just found my button." She turned toward the desk and retrieved a safety pin.

"Well, I guess I'll leave you two to your work," Mabel said, as if she didn't believe for one moment that was what they were about to do.

"It was good seeing you again," Malcolm said, barely able to contain his amusement.

"Give my love to the family." Mabel glanced back at Gloria, shook her head and made her exit.

"Well," he said. "I guess that means it's just you and me."

"Apparently." She mimicked his awkward smile. "Let's get started. We've already wasted enough time."

He couldn't agree more. The sooner he got out of there, the better. He turned and moved toward the first line of file cabinets near the window, pulled opened the top drawer and quickly started shoving files into the closest container.

"No. No," Gloria said, rushing over. "Some material will need to stay here for the new…I mean…"

"It's all right," Malcolm said, rescuing her from tripping over her tongue again. "I know what you mean—for whoever is going to take my father's place."

"No one could ever take Harmon's place."

Jealousy stabbed Malcolm and robbed him of his breath, although he agreed wholeheartedly with Gloria's proclamation. Not for the first time, Malcolm wondered whether Gloria's feelings transcended the boss-and-employee relationship.

She flashed something that was obviously meant to be a smile, but ended up looking like perhaps her shoes were pinching the hell out of her feet. "I'm sorry. It all still seems so…surreal."

He nodded. A moment of silence flowed between

them while his eyes lowered and he damned the safety pin she'd used to close her blouse. He slammed his eyes shut and chanted in his head: *focus, focus, focus.*

"All right, Ms. Kingsley. In addition to the bookshelves, desk and walls, why don't you tell me *exactly* how you want this part done?"

"Well," she said, straightening her back. "I want you to carefully go through each folder and remove only the personal files or pet projects. Then I want you to use these dividers and tabs I purchased—" she reached for the stack of office supplies he'd missed "—and label everything and place them into the containers in alphabetical order."

"You're kidding."

"No." She frowned again. "It'll make it easier for your family to sift through."

"It'll also take all night," he grumbled, glancing around the office.

"What?"

"I said, 'Yes, ma'am.'" He made a mock military salute.

Gloria's eyes narrowed. "Look. I'm just trying to be helpful."

"Of course you are," he said with more sarcasm than he intended.

Gloria glared, drew a deep breath and then

turned away. "I'll start on the desk," she said with a strained calm.

Again, Malcolm's gaze was drawn to her heavenly backside as she made her way across the room and then planted herself in his father's old leather chair.

Instead of getting straight to work, she rechecked her safety pin.

Malcolm barely turned away in time. It wouldn't do to continually get caught staring, but he felt her gaze rest on him. He sucked in his invisible tummy and straightened his shoulders so that she could get a good look and…what? Did he want her to like what she was seeing?

Soon her eyes trailed away and a strange, awkward silence enveloped the room. An hour passed, and Malcolm felt he'd made about as much progress as a turtle sprinting a hundred-yard dash. Periodically, Malcolm would finger his open collar or wipe at imaginary sweat beads. He continued to feel as if he was wilting beneath a desert sun, though the thermostat read a cool seventy-four degrees.

"Are you sure this thing is working?" he asked, tapping the small square box.

"It's working," she answered without glancing up. She, apparently, had no trouble concentrating on her work.

When Malcolm reached the bottom of the first file cabinet, he pulled open the drawer and blinked in surprise. Malcolm pulled out a glass picture frame, almost a mirror image of the one of his father at the bottom of Malcolm's DVD cabinet—right down to the spiderweb cracks in the center. It was a picture of Malcolm graduating from Morehouse College. His father's arms were wrapped around Malcolm's shoulders, while his chin and chest were lifted high with pride.

A pain in his heart caused a few tears to trickle from the corners of his eyes. Here was the proof of his father's disappointment in him. The only photo of father and son was buried in a drawer.

"It's not what you think," Gloria said.

Malcolm whirled around to find Gloria behind him, breaching his privacy. "How do you know what I think?"

He shoved the picture into the container and moved to the next filing cabinet.

"Your father pulled that picture out every day," she said softly.

"I don't want to talk about it," he said.

"Malcolm—"

"I *said* I don't want to talk about it." He slammed the top file cabinet closed.

Gloria jumped.

"I need to get some air," he said, and stormed past her. More than anything, he was embarrassed for losing control and once again lashing out at her. But, hell, she was the only one around.

"Why don't we stop and go get some dinner?" she suggested, striding after him and grabbing his wrist. "You need a break."

"No. I want to hurry and get this over with," he said. "I just need a quick breather."

"C'mon," she said. "You need to eat. I need to eat. Let's just go somewhere and grab something—and we can talk."

Talk. Couldn't she see that was the last thing he wanted to do?

"I'm not hungry," he lied. Just then, his stomach released a long winding growl. For a few seconds, he tried to hold on to his stern expression.

Gloria's beautiful full lips were the first to split into a wide smile before her laughter erupted from the center of her chest.

After a few seconds, Malcolm joined her.

"Do you still like Chinese?" she asked. "There's a nice place a few miles from here."

He sighed, hesitating.

"It's on me," she added.

He chuckled. "*I'll* pay."

"I tell you what. Let's make it Dutch," she

countered. "That way no one will mistake it for being a date."

"A date? Me and you?" Malcolm laughed. "Trust me. No one will make that mistake."

Chapter 4

Gloria couldn't wait to get out of the office. Despite the spacious size, it felt as if they were literally on top of each other and walking on eggshells. Dinner, she hoped, would relax Malcolm a bit more. She needed him to loosen up in order for him to be receptive to what she had in mind.

The Bamboo House was dark when they entered. The only lighting flickered from tiny wicks nestled in small red candleholders placed in the center of each table in sconces on the walls.

"Ah, Ms. Kingsley," Samira, the hostess, greeted her. "So nice to see you again. I'm so sorry. I read in the paper what happened to Harmon. It was a shock, no?"

Gloria nodded while the small woman grabbed hold of her hand.

"How are you?" Samira asked with genuine concern. "I know we're definitely going to miss seeing you two in here."

Malcolm's gaze shot to Gloria, his brows launched high. "You and my father came here often?"

"Often?" Samira chimed. "They came here two or three times a week with their noses buried in paperwork." Then as if finally catching what Malcolm said, Samira dropped Gloria's hand and turned her attention toward him. "Harmon was your father?" She gazed up at him. "Ah, yes. I see the resemblance now." Her smile turned flirtatious. "You're very handsome like your father."

Malcolm smiled. "Thank you. You're too kind."

Samira glanced at Gloria and winked. "You better hold on to your heart with this one. He just might steal it."

Gloria's face burned; she had to touch it to make sure it hadn't melted off.

Malcolm coughed, choking back his own laughter.

"This way," Samira sang, grabbing two menus. "Will it be just the two of you?"

"Yes," Gloria answered.

"Would you like your and Harmon's regular table? It's available."

"Uh," she said, stalling.

"That will be fine," Malcolm answered, carefully keeping his eyes away from Gloria's.

Gloria fell in line behind the hostess as she led them toward the back of the restaurant. It might have been her imagination, but she swore she felt Malcolm's heavy gaze trained on the back of her head. Was he already regretting coming here with her?

Most likely.

"Have a good evening," Samira said, setting the menus down on their table. "Your server will be with you shortly."

Malcolm and Gloria thanked the hostess and slid into opposing sides of a large booth.

Gloria tried her best not to jump or react when Malcolm's knees and legs bumped and brushed against her own. She needed to get it together before she looked like a Mexican jumping bean.

"Well, this is certainly cozy," Malcolm said, finally settling into his seat. "I can see why this was your and Dad's favorite spot."

Gloria's head snapped up. "What is that supposed to mean?"

He shrugged. "Nothing."

"No," she countered. Her eyes narrowed. "It definitely meant something."

Malcolm met her gaze dead-on.

"Is there something you want to say to me?" she challenged.

Silence.

"Go ahead. What is it?"

He shook his head. "Nothing. Forget it." He picked up his menu.

"No." She snatched the menu from his hand and slapped it back down onto the table. "We need to have this out. Go ahead. Ask me."

"All right, then," he said, leaning forward. "Were you in love with my father?"

Gloria drew a deep breath despite the fact that she was expecting the question. Her shoulders squared while her back morphed into an iron rod.

Malcolm cocked his head. "Maybe you two got together for more than just…business dinners?"

She shook her head, disappointed in just how little Malcolm thought of his father and of her, for that matter. "I'm not going to lie," she said evenly. "I loved your father."

Malcolm's jaw hardened.

"But I was not *in* love with him," she clarified. "It was strictly business between us. He was my mentor and my hero."

"Hero?" he spat. "Not too many employees think of their bosses as heroes."

"Everyone that worked for your father did," she retorted. "I believe you did, too, at one time," she added as a sucker punch.

Malcolm's chin came up as he sat up straight.

"Frankly, I can't believe you'd think such a thing. I had nothing but the highest regard for your father. I respected him, myself *and* his marriage." Even as she confessed, she watched waves of doubt wash over Malcolm's stony features. It only angered her more.

"Why is it that you're so determined to think the worst of your father? Surely it's not because he didn't support that *one* bill?"

"*That* one bill…" Malcolm clamped his mouth shut and forced himself to calm down. "You know what? I think coming here was a mistake."

It was Gloria's turn to cock her head and stare. "You have a habit of doing that."

"A habit of doing what?"

"Running away." Gloria leaned back and folded her arms. "You haven't noticed?" She smirked. "When things get a little hot, you always seem to need to run out…for air."

Malcolm leaned back and mimicked her pose. "Is that right?"

"It makes me wonder if you have what it takes to…"

Brows sloped unevenly, he asked, "Have what it takes to do what?"

"Nothing," she said blithely. "Forget I said anything."

"No." He shook his head. "Obviously, *you* have something you want to say, as well."

Their waiter, Quon, a tall, lanky Asian with an obvious aversion to smiling, arrived and Gloria breathed a sigh of relief.

"Ah, Ms. Kingsley. Nice to see you here again," he said, setting two empty plastic cups before them and then filling them with a pitcher of iced water. "Are you ready to order?"

"Yes," Gloria said.

"No," Malcolm countered, and then added, "Could you please give us a few more minutes?"

Gloria's brows stretched high. Maybe she wasn't off the hook just yet.

"As you wish, sir," Quon said, sliding away from their table.

"You've never struck me as someone who liked to play games," Malcolm said, the moment they were alone. "But I'm starting to feel like an unprotected king in the center of a chess game."

Gloria shrugged her shoulder and tried her best

to look as innocent as possible. "I don't know what you mean."

"Don't you?" He laughed. "You tell me to come help pack my father's office, assuring me it will only take a couple of hours when you and I both know it would be, at minimum, an all-nighter. Then of course there is this dinner—"

"Well. You make it sound like I held a gun to your head. Is being alone with me so terrible?" she snapped. "Maybe I just wanted…to talk. Share stories about how great a man your father was or how much he meant to me and the other staffers. I was a fan of your father's long before I started working for him. He was a powerful speaker and he campaigned for health-care reform long before the number of uninsured reached crisis numbers. I was thrilled when Senator Cayman recommended me to Harmon. I just…" After a few seconds with struggling for the right words, she clamped her mouth shut, but her lips continued to tremble and tears burned the backs of her eyes.

Gloria drew a deep breath and tried to pull herself together. It wasn't supposed to be this hard.

At the first sight of tears shimmering in Gloria's eyes, Malcolm felt as if he'd been punched in the gut. Obviously, the woman was still grieving, and here he was…

He sighed. "Look. So far it seems I've spent half the night apologizing to you for my behavior. Why don't we just…start over?"

She glanced at him and wiped a tear before it broke free from the mesh of her eyelashes.

"For real," he assured her. "This time, I'll be on my best behavior." He placed his hand over his heart. "I promise."

Finally, Gloria smiled and nodded.

Their waiter returned. "Have you two made your decisions?"

"Hmm." Malcolm grabbed his menu and quickly perused the items. "What's good here?"

"You should really try the Hunan chicken with black mushrooms," Gloria suggested. "It was your father's…I mean…" Her words trailed off.

Malcolm offered her a small smile. "I know what you mean. And you know what?" He handed the menu over to the waiter. "I think that's exactly what I'll have."

She returned the smile and surprised him by ordering the Mongolian barbecue beef. She might be a small woman but she had a healthy appetite. He liked that.

"Very good selection," Quon intoned, his lips still a flat line as he scurried off toward the kitchen.

Being alone with Gloria—with anyone, really—

was the very thing Malcolm had tried to avoid since the news of his father's death.

He wasn't ready to be the shoulder to cry on. How could he deal with other people's grief when he didn't know how to deal with his own? However, the longer he stayed in Gloria's presence, the more he was able to see through her thin veneer. She wanted what everyone wanted—for him to open up.

And maybe—just maybe—he wanted that, too.

As he witnessed her struggle, a small part of him caved. "I loved my father," Malcolm said suddenly.

Gloria lifted her shimmering gaze.

"I don't want you to think I stopped loving him," he added softly, and then cleared his throat. "I still love him. It's just that our relationship in the past couple of years was…complicated."

"Most are."

"Oh?" He arched his brow. "I've never heard you talk about your family."

"When have you ever been around?" she asked.

"I guess that's a good point," Malcolm said with a tilt of his head. "Are you close to your father?"

Gloria's eyes lowered to the table while she gave a firm shake of her head.

Malcolm wondered how it was possible she could judge him when she apparently had issues with her own father. Yet, he bit back the comment.

As if she'd heard his private thoughts, she responded, "Trust me. My father wasn't half the man Harmon Braddock was. He was a drunk and an abuser. The happiest day in my life was when he walked right out of it."

Stunned, Malcolm remained silent. Finally, he slowly nodded in understanding, but he was more curious than ever. During their quiet spells, Malcolm couldn't help but reflect over his childhood once again, zeroing in on the number of Little League and college games his father did make time for, and the number of father-and-son camping events he and Ty enjoyed despite their father's busy schedule. Harmon Braddock had a way of making his sons feel ten feet tall, always bragging to anyone who'd stand still long enough to listen.

The truth of the matter was that Malcolm had had a wonderful childhood.

That annoying stinging in the back of Malcolm's eyes returned as well as the mountainous lump clogging his windpipe, but thank God, Quon returned, rescuing him from his emotions with their dinner orders.

"Can I get you anything else?" the waiter asked, setting their plates before them.

After they assured him they had everything they needed, Quon, once again, slipped away from the table.

For a time they ate in silence before Malcolm blurted, "I keep thinking that at any moment I'm going to wake up and find out that the past week has just been a dream." He stared into his plate. "A nightmare, really."

Gloria said nothing.

"It's true what they say," he said. "Regret has a way of killing you softly. There were so many times I wanted to call."

She reached across the table and covered his hand. The warmth of her touch traveled up the length of his arm.

"Don't beat yourself up. I know the disagreement between you two spiraled out of control, but the love remained. That much was evident."

"But did he know?" Malcolm questioned.

"Of course he did." Gloria nodded. "And you know something else? He was extremely proud of you—your intelligence, convictions and even your passion." She squeezed his hand tighter. "He was proud of all his children, and if you don't mind me saying so, he had every right to be."

Her encouraging words were just the balm Malcolm needed. He only prayed they were the truth. After all, every child wants their parents to be proud of them.

Gloria chuckled and drew Malcolm out of his melancholy.

"What's so funny?" His lips curled, ready to join in on the joke.

"You probably don't know this," she said. "But once upon a time, your father tried to hook us up together."

His laughter came easily at that revelation. "You're joking."

"Hilarious, isn't it?" She shook her head and released his hand. "The first few months I started working for him, he wouldn't stop telling me how much of a *fine* catch you were and how a woman would be crazy not to cast her net in your direction." She chuckled. "He actually said *'cast her net.'* He shoved so many dinner invitations my way, I ran out of excuses to why I couldn't come."

Malcolm choked on his food.

"Are you all right?" she asked when it started to sound like he was trying to hack up a lung.

He bobbed his head, reached for his iced water.

She watched him through growing concern until he finally held up a finger and said, "I'm okay."

"What happened? Went down the wrong pipe?"

"Something like that." He cleared his throat and

favored her with a smile. "You mean all those times you showed up at my parents' house for Sunday dinner and holiday meals were because my dad was trying to play Cupid?"

She returned his smile. "After we met at that one fund-raiser, I told him not to bother. We mixed as well as oil and water."

"Now, who is the oil in this scenario?"

Gloria waved a finger, letting him know she wasn't going to allow him to bait her into an argument. "The point is that we're completely wrong for each other," she stressed.

Malcolm hadn't intended to, but he frowned. What was it about him that she found rejection-able? He straightened his chair and averted his gaze.

"Not that I don't find you attractive," she rushed to say as she sensed his bruised ego. "I do."

He glanced up.

"I mean—any woman would. It's just, um, personality-wise, we don't mesh."

"Because you don't like men with intelligence, convictions and—what was it—passion?"

"Right." She blinked. "Wait. I mean—"

Malcolm's head rocked back while his chest rumbled with laughter. "Please. Please. Let's quit before you *really* hurt my feelings."

Gloria pressed her lips together, but her eyes

seemed to dance with the candlelight. "I do have a way of putting my foot in my mouth, don't I?"

Leaning over to the side, he squinted under the table and blinked. "You better be careful. Those jokers are big."

"Ha. Ha." She rolled her eyes. "You got me back. Can we eat now?"

"No, really. What size are those puppies—eleven, twelve?"

"Eight." She kicked him.

"Ow." He laughed.

"Serves you right, saying my feet are big. The real question is what size are *your* feet? You know what they say about the size of a man's feet." She leaned over and glanced under the table herself, but the laughter died on her lips.

"Satisfied?" he asked.

She sat up, her face as red as the candleholder. "We better finish eating."

"Are you sure?" A devilish grin spread across his face before he commenced eating. This time, the silence was more comfortable while they snuck glances at each other and smiled whenever they were caught.

Maybe Gloria Kingsley wasn't so bad after all.

Chapter 5

Malcolm arrived home at midnight.

Exhausted didn't describe it—more like he was bone weary. His eyes were dry from looking at too much paperwork. His back ached from loading one too many tubs of law books. The last thing he wanted to do now was unload it all and carry it up to his apartment. That would have to be another project for another time. For the time being he kept everything locked in his SUV. Tomorrow, he promised himself, he'd carry everything out to the family estate.

If not, then maybe the day after.

He slipped his key into the apartment's lock, pushed the door open and felt a sense of relief when he stepped into the apartment's darkness. First pit stop: the kitchen. Malcolm grabbed the last beer in the fridge and made a mental note to pick up a case while he was out tomorrow. His next stop was the living room, where he tumbled onto the leather couch. He caught view of the blinking red light on his answer machine.

Twelve messages.

Even before he hit the play button, he knew who the callers were.

"Malcolm?" Shawnie's voice filtered through the speakerphone. "Are you there? Pick up if you're there." After a long pause, she sighed and continued. "Well, I was just calling to check on you. No one in the family has heard from you and…well, it's really not the time to be alone, Malcolm. We all need you. We love you." Another long silence and then, "Call me."

Malcolm groaned while he slid a hand over his face.

The machine beeped and played the next message.

"Malcolm?" Tyson's steel baritone punched through the apartment's stillness. "C'mon, man. I know you're there. Pick up." After a few beats of silence his brother went on, "Look, man. I know you're going through a rough time. Things being the way they were with you and Dad and all, but give me a call. We need to talk. And if you don't feel like talking to me the least you can do is call Mom. She's worried about you. Hit me up on my cell when you get this message."

The calls alternated between Shawnie and Ty. Both of their voices thickened with concern each time he didn't answer the phone. Malcolm was instantly sorry for making everyone worry. That had not been his intention.

On the last message, Malcolm's heart tried to squeeze its way out of his chest when his mother's wearied voice entered the room.

"Malcolm, baby. Are you there? Baby, please pick up the phone."

Silence.

"All right, baby. You must not be there. I was just going through some old family photo albums. You keep drifting across my mind. Baby, I'm getting a little worried about you. I haven't heard or seen you since the funeral. Give me a call."

At first Malcolm had no intentions of calling any of them back this late, but there was something about his mother's voice that tugged at his soul and made him pick up the phone and punch in her number. Even as he listened to the phone ring, he chastised himself for calling so late. She was probably asleep, he reasoned, and even hoped.

"I'll call her tomorrow," he said, and started to hang up.

"Hello?" His mother's soft southern twang filtered over the line. "Malcolm?"

"Hey, Mom," he answered with an aloofness he didn't feel. "How are you?"

"Actually, that's the question I wanted to ask you. Are you all right, baby?"

No was what he wanted to say, but he had some sense to at least pretend he was keeping it together. "Yeah. I'm all right. How are you holding up?"

"Well…I guess I'm doing about as well as can be expected." Her voice grew heavier with each word. "I wish you were around more, though. Why haven't you been by?"

Even though Malcolm had a list of reasons on standby, he couldn't get himself to spit out any of them. Mainly because when it came right down to it, there was no *good* reason why he hadn't been the man his mother needed him to be.

"Trust me, Mama. I wouldn't have made good company." Her chuckle surprised him.

"Well, none of us are good company right now," she said, and then sobered a bit. "However, there's strength in numbers. I've taught you that."

He nodded against the phone as if she could see him. "I know. Tell you what. I promise to make it there by tomorrow."

"Promise?"

"Yeah. I promise."

Evelyn's voice immediately strengthened. "Then I guess I better call off your brother's plan of kidnapping you and dragging you here against your will."

Malcolm laughed. "Is that right?"

"Well, he was worried, baby. We all are."

"There's no need to worry, Mama. I'm all right. I spent the night at dad's office with Gloria, packing up some of his things."

"Oh?" She perked up. "And how is Gloria doing? You know, I always did like her."

Malcolm couldn't believe his ears. "Not you, too," he groaned.

"What?" she asked. However, her tone belied her innocent act.

"Gloria told me over dinner how Dad used to try to set us up."

"Dinner?"

"A quick meal…as friends."

"A dinner—a date. Same thing."

"Not the same thing."

"Who paid?"

"Dutch."

"Malcolm Braddock, I thought I raised you better. A man should never allow a woman to pay for a meal. It's ungentlemanly."

"Mom, leave Cupid's bow alone. It's never going to happen. At least Dad finally realized that."

"Oh, please. You're giving your father way too much credit. You think he noticed things like that? Why, I thought she was the sweetest thing the first time I laid eyes on her. I was the one always pushing for Harmon to extend her dinner invitations. Of course, getting you here was damn near impossible, too. I don't know if I've ever told you this, dear, but you really do have a stubborn streak."

"Stubborn?" he repeated, as if insulted.

"Oh, don't start," she said. "You come by it honestly. Your father knew how to dig in his heels, as well." She chuckled, and then cleared her throat. "To tell you the truth, it was one of the good things I liked about him."

"That's the first time I heard that one."

"If he hadn't been so hardheaded, then he would have accepted my no the first time he proposed to me." She laughed. "And I would have missed out on forty years of a wonderful marriage and three beautiful children. Your father gave me a wonderful life. I'll always love him for that. But it's more than time for grandbabies."

"Oh, boy. Don't start that again." He chuckled, leaning back into the sofa. He was actually enjoying their conversation.

"It's true," Evelyn insisted.

"Uh-huh."

"What? It's not like I'm asking for much. I want to see all my children happily married and producing beautiful babies. Now that Gloria—I bet she could make some adorable children."

"Whoa. Whoa. Whoa." He sat up; his laughter rumbled into the phone. "You've gone from trying to call an innocent dinner a date to now having us with kids."

"C'mon," she needled. "You can't tell me you don't find Gloria attractive."

"Attraction is not the issue. Compatibility is. Gloria and I—"

"You and Gloria have a lot in common."

"Are you sure *Dad* was the hardheaded one?" Malcolm asked.

"Ha. Ha. I know what I know—and I know Gloria Kingsley is the perfect woman for you."

Malcolm laughed, though clearly he was the only one who found the statement funny. "It's never going to happen," he stated firmly.

"Why not?" his mother challenged; her voice carried a smile.

Because I'm not like my father.

"Well?" Evelyn pressed.

Malcolm cleared his throat. "Let's just say that I'm not what she's looking for."

Determined not to spend another day moping around the apartment, Malcolm rose early Tuesday morning and decided that it was time to return to the land of the living. He thought about driving out to the family estate to deliver the items packed from his father's office. He knew he'd promised his mother, but he couldn't bring himself to do it.

Not just yet.

Instead, he climbed out of bed, showered and made his way over to his office at the Arc Foundation.

"Mr. Braddock!" Paula Heizman blinked up at him when he breezed into his office suite. "What are you doing here?"

"Last time I checked I still worked here," he said, managing to ease a smile onto his face without breaking his stride.

Paula followed. "But you said you'd be out this week."

"I changed my mind," he said. "I need to stay busy."

His assistant stared wide-eyed at him.

"What's the matter, Ms. Heizman? Did I ruin

some big party you guys had planned in my absence? You hadn't hired a bunch of male strippers to come and perform while everyone should be working, did you?"

Paula's creamy white skin turned into a bright shade of pink. "For the last time, my sister hired that stripper for my fortieth birthday."

"Uh-huh," he deliberately said in a dubious tone just to deepen her embarrassment.

"Honestly, I don't know why I bother," she mumbled with a roll of her eyes, and then made a quick exit from his office.

Malcolm chuckled in her wake and finally dropped into the cheap office chair behind his desk. There was a rush of excitement at seeing the stack of papers overflowing his in-box. Finally there was something that could get his mind off his troubles. The first hour breezed by, but the second crawled at a snail's pace, and by the third hour, he was more than ready to call it a day.

"Knock. Knock." Paula floated into the office.

"Yes, Paula?"

"I have Orville Roark on the phone. He wants to know whether you're still coming to the Texas Children's Cancer Center fund-raiser."

Malcolm blinked up at her. "When is that again?"

"Tomorrow night."

He hesitated, wondering if he was truly up to schmoozing with a crowd of inquiring minds.

"No pressure," Paula assured him. "I'm sure he'll understand if you're not up to it."

Malcolm smiled, appreciating Paula for her understanding—but he was more than aware of the importance of this particular fund-raiser. The Texas Children's Cancer Center was one of the largest health-care charities for pediatric treatment and research. All patients were accepted regardless of the families' ability to pay; but in order for the center to operate, it relied heavily on city and state leaders to organize fund-raisers, dinners, tournaments and even door-to-door begging.

Still, he wasn't sure he was ready for a night of endless handshakes, plastic smiles and needling questions. "Give my apologies, but tell him the Arc Foundation will still be making that financial contribution from the concert we had last month."

"Will do," Paula said solemnly, and then popped her head back out of the office.

Malcolm slumped back into his chair, hoping Orville really would understand. "Just a few more days," he promised himself, "and I should be back to my old self." His heart squeezed in response to the lie. He would never be his old self again.

Before that troubling thought had time to settle, there was another knock on his door. "Come in," he said, simultaneously reaching for another stack of paperwork.

"Hey. You're here."

Malcolm looked up—stunned to see Gloria in his door frame and smiling.

"I hope I didn't catch you at a bad time?" She stepped inside and glanced around his sparse office space.

Malcolm climbed onto his feet. "What are you doing here?"

Her smile widened. "Have you noticed you ask me that question a lot?"

"No," he admitted. "But I have noticed you make it a habit of showing up at unexpected places."

To that charge, she simply shrugged and then cast her attention to the photographs of children the Arc Foundation had been able to help since its inception. As Gloria moved around the room, Malcolm's chest puffed out with pride. "This is your first time here, isn't it?"

Gloria nodded, now perusing the awards and plaques gracing one side of the office. "Very impressive," she said.

His chest puffed a little higher. "Thank you." He eyeballed her crisp business pantsuit, inky black with a cotton-candy-pink blouse. Her beautiful golden eyes were encased by square-framed black glasses while her hair was pulled up and secured in a tight bun. Beauty and brains—a heady combination.

"You know your father followed your work religiously."

"Really." Malcolm returned to his chair.

"Yes, really," she said, eyeing him. "Surely that doesn't come as a surprise?"

Malcolm tried not to groan, but he couldn't help it. He'd come to work to get away from ghosts. "Is there something you need, Gloria? I have a lot of work to catch up on."

"Actually, I came to ask you for a favor."

He frowned. "What sort of favor?"

"Well, nothing too strenuous that will take up much of your time."

"No offense, but you're not exactly a good judge when it comes to time management. The last two-hour project shockingly took all night."

"Sorry I interrupted your previously scheduled pity party to do something that needed to be done," she responded smoothly with a smile.

Malcolm bit back a retort and instead asked his question again. "What do you want, Gloria?"

Gloria took a deep breath and widened her smile a bit. "I was going through your father's calendar and saw he was scheduled to attend a fund-raiser tomorrow night."

Malcolm struggled to hide his smile. "A fund-raiser?"

"Yes. For the Texas Children's Cancer Center." She walked to his desk. "I know it's short notice and I know how much you've taken to being walled up in your apartment lately, but it really is an important function. One I know your father was looking forward to."

"Is that right?" he asked, unable to contain his sarcasm. More likely his father was just interested in doing his prerequisite amount of "face" charity work to satisfy the press.

"Orville Roark was very instrumental in lighting a serious torch under your father. He contributed generously. I'm surprised Mr. Roark hasn't reached out to the Arc Foundation. Their center seems to be just the thing your organization would jump on."

Malcolm recognized the question buried in the statement and he decided that it would be best to steer clear of her fishing expedition.

"Malcolm, I know it's a lot to ask right now, but could you please attend in your father's place? It would mean so much to me if you did."

"To you?" he asked. His chin shot upward.

"It would be great for the Arc Foundation, as well," Gloria reasoned. "I've been reading up on you."

"Stay up all night on the Internet, did you?"

"No. I told you your father kept tabs on you. Who do you think gathered the information?"

"I'm sure somewhere in there I'm supposed be flattered you've been spying on me."

"You know what?" she asked, crossing her arms. "I think you'd be surprised just how much you and your father have in common."

"So you keep telling me."

"And it's true." Gloria leaned forward and covered his hand with her own. "Come to the fund-raiser."

He sighed, milking the situation since he liked the feel of her hand.

"Please," she added.

Sighing, he felt no remorse in not telling her he'd already been invited to the fund-raiser. "I don't know," he hedged. "I'll have to dust off my tux."

"Or buy a new one," she suggested.

Malcolm's eyebrows crashed together. "What's wrong with my tux?"

"It would be a shorter list if you asked me what was right with it. When did you buy that thing?"

"My mother bought that tux."

"When—for the prom?"

"Ha. Ha." He slid his hand from beneath hers. "Sorry, I'm more of a jeans and T-shirt kind of guy."

"Amen," she mumbled. "I tell you what. Why don't I take you shopping?"

"Come again?"

"You heard me," Gloria said, her eyes sweeping across him. "A man never gets a second chance to make a first impression. How about we go after work today?"

"I don't need you to hold my hand to go shopping."

In a flash, Gloria retrieved her BlackBerry from her purse. "I get off at five—will that be a problem?" she asked, ignoring his protest.

"Gloria, I *said* I can buy my own suit."

"Oh, I'm sure you can but, um, you shouldn't."

"Excuse me?"

"Instead of taking the chance of you showing up in something like the suit you were wearing when I first met you, I think I should step in and help."

He blinked. "You know, you have this way of sounding like you're being nice when you're really insulting a person."

Her smile grew wider. "Really? I'll work on that. I'll come pick you up."

The woman was determined to have her way.

"Great." She clapped her hands together and turned toward the door.

"I didn't say yes," he said.

"But you want to," she said. "Don't worry, I'll be your date if you can't find someone on short notice."

He frowned.

"Well, it's not a date-date," she clarified.

"Oh, really?" He leaned back in his chair. "When someone asks someone out, by definition that's called a date."

"It's not a date," she stressed.

He stretched his brows high. "Then what would you call it?"

"We're two friends attending a very important fund-raiser for a great cause."

"Friends?"

Gloria's back straightened. "Acquaintances?"

Malcolm's eyes lowered to the curve of her waist. "I don't know," he hesitated. "It still sort of sounds like a date."

Gloria folded her arms, her patience thin.

He frowned and shook his head as if he was still deliberating.

"C'mon. Surely, going out with me isn't all that bad," she said sneakily.

"You're not helping your case."

"What? Are you scared of me?" she challenged, stalking toward his desk like a cougar locking in on her next prey. "Maybe that's the real reason you're always trying to run away. You're scared of little ole me."

"Hardly."

"Prove it."

"I don't have to prove—"

"Chicken." She crossed her arms and smiled snidely.

"I'm not—"

"B-gwak! B-gwak!"

Malcolm frowned.

"Just trying to talk to you in your native language."

"Very mature."

Gloria made a few more clucking sounds.

"All right. All right. I'll go," he agreed, shaking his head and wondering for the first time if perhaps Ms. Kingsley wasn't dealing with a full deck.

"Great." She straightened with a victorious grin and then headed toward the door. "It's a date. I'll pick you up this afternoon around five-thirty for your tux fitting."

Chapter 6

Malcolm couldn't have concentrated on work if his life depended on it.

A date? What the hell did she mean "it's a date"? He shook his head and tried to concentrate on the words scattered across the thick stack of paperwork before him. "It's not a date," he mumbled. "If anything, it's just like she said earlier—two friends...acquaintances—attending a very important fund-raiser for a great cause."

Again, Malcolm shook his head. This was just another example of how much his life had turned upside down in the past week. What was once black was now white. What was once white was now…a date?

Leaning back in his chair, Malcolm contemplated the situation, still unable to shake the feeling that Gloria Kingsley was up to something. What—he had no idea. But it was definitely *something*.

For the rest of the day, Malcolm watched the clock. A few times, he actually held his watch to his ear to make sure the damn thing was still ticking. When he realized what he was doing, he questioned his continued anxiousness when it came to seeing Gloria.

Maybe it wasn't her—but his curiosity of what she had up her sleeve. He nodded. He liked that idea better.

At precisely five o'clock, Paula stuck her head back into the office and told him she was calling it a day.

"Is there anything else I can get for you?" she asked, sliding her purse strap over her shoulder.

"No, no. I have everything under control," he said.

Paula nodded and continued to eye him strangely.

"Really," he stressed.

"I know you said you just want to stay busy," she said, "but be careful not to overdo it."

The note of concern in her voice touched him. "I'll keep that in mind," he said.

Paula nodded and then backed out of the door.

Once he was alone again, he stood from his chair

and walked over to his office window, where he watched a great number of the Arc Foundation's employees and volunteers filter out of the building. He wasn't aware of thinking of anything. He was content to just watch.

Malcolm did, however, become aware of a growing sense of unfairness. How was it that the sun continued to rise and set without his father being in it? How was his mother supposed to go on without her husband of four decades? How was he supposed to be forgiven when his dad was no longer around to do the forgiving?

He glanced over his shoulder and back at the clock sitting on his desk.

Five-fifteen. He knew his mother would be disappointed that he hadn't come by, but he could always blame it on Gloria needing his help.

Maybe she wouldn't come, Malcolm hoped when his thoughts traveled back to having to attend the black-tie event. Heck, he might even be able to talk Tyson and Felicia into going in his place.

The memory of Gloria descending a flight of stairs at that long-ago fund-raiser in an amazing black, backless gown was strong enough to stall Malcolm's breathing. Maybe if he were lucky, she would wear something similar to that again.

Five-twenty.

Beautiful as Gloria might be, he doubted they could declare a truce for an entire night. She just had too smart a mouth for her own good.

Malcolm turned back toward the window just as another memory of Gloria crawling on all fours drifted across his mind—in particular, the way her ample bottom was perked up in his direction.

"Sorry I'm late," Gloria said, breezing into his office and flashing him a smile.

Malcolm glanced at the clock and saw that she was actually five minutes early.

"Are you ready to go?" she asked, scanning her watch and fretting as though she was running on a tight schedule.

"Er, um…about the fund-raiser," Malcolm started.

"Please tell me you're not going to try to back out on me now. I've already made confirmations that you'd attend. You should have told me that you had already been invited," she scolded.

He actually flushed under her soft reprimand.

Gloria marched over to his desk and grabbed his jacket, then rushed over toward him to help him put it on. "Don't worry. You won't have to stay long. Just put in a little face time, write a check and we're out," she said as if the matter was already settled.

Malcolm started to protest again, but she immediately cut him off.

"C'mon. C'mon. We have an appointment with Jose over at Anderson's. He was kind enough to squeeze you in at the last minute for your measurements."

Sensing he wasn't going to win the argument, Malcolm slid one arm through the sleeve of his jacket and she buzzed around him so he could glide into the second.

"Great. We'll take my car," she said, leading him toward a blue BMW Mini Cooper.

Malcolm stopped and stared.

"What's wrong?" she asked as she opened her car door.

"Um." He cocked his head. "I don't think I'm going to fit into that matchbox. Don't you have a *real* car?"

Gloria jabbed a hand to her waist. "It *is* a real car. It's roomier than it looks."

"Somehow I doubt that." He headed toward the passenger door, certain that his knees were going to be planted near his chin. "You know I don't mind driving. My SUV is right over there."

"Will you stop complaining and get in the car?"

"Yes, ma'am." He gave her a mock salute and climbed into her toy car. To his surprise the inside was roomy, saving him from being jammed into the dashboard.

"See? I told you."

Malcolm swallowed his moan. Did she always have to gloat?

However, the one thing Malcolm was *not* prepared for was Gloria Kingsley's driving—if one wanted to call it that. Her zigzagging between cars, speeding up and then slamming on her brakes while she tailgated like Stevie Wonder behind the wheel was enough to give him motion sickness.

Horns blared from every direction, and to his shock, Gloria flashed more than a handful of birds and trash-talked her way through rush-hour traffic.

Who *was* this woman?

"Where in the hell did you get your driver's license?"

Red sparks flashed from her eyes. "What's wrong with my driving?" she asked, once again slamming on her brakes and stopping less than inch from the car before them.

Malcolm's eyes bulged as his seat belt dug into his shoulder, locking him in place but causing havoc on his internal organs. "Maybe you should pull over and let me drive."

"Why? I'm a good driver. I've never gotten a ticket or been in an accident. So you just sit over there and enjoy the ride."

It would have been easier to do if he was on some crazy ride at Disneyland and his life wasn't in danger. As it was, he found himself whispering a few prayers as they made their way across town. Every other second he was hollering for her to "watch out" or "stop" or "slow down."

By the time she whipped the Mini Cooper into the strip mall they were both irritable and angry.

"I swear you have to be the worse backseat driver I've ever had," she complained.

Malcolm ignored her as he battled the urge to drop to his knees and kiss the concrete.

"Oh, c'mon. You big baby," Gloria chastised. She slid her purse strap over her shoulder and marched toward the building.

Malcolm shook his head and followed.

"Ah, Ms. Kingsley," Jose Hernandez greeted her, sweeping his arms wide and allowing her to step into his embrace, where he kissed each side of her face.

Malcolm frowned at the short, squat man and ignored any possibility that the knot in his stomach had anything to do with jealousy.

"Thank you so much for taking us at the last minute," Gloria cooed.

"For you," Jose said, "anything." He then shifted his attention toward Malcolm. "It's nice to see you again, Mr. Braddock."

Malcolm frowned.

"I fitted you for your brother's wedding some years back."

"Ah," Malcolm said, nodding and accepting the man's offered hand. "It's good seeing you again."

Jose kept nodding, but his lips tilted into a frown. "You know we sell more than just tuxedos. We carry the best suits in the state."

Gloria chuckled. "Actually, Jose, Malcolm here is more of a jeans-and-T-shirt kind of guy. If it's real fancy he might be able to find a pair of khaki pants somewhere."

Malcolm would have responded if he hadn't been captivated by her girlish, flirtatious giggle, and he couldn't help but smile in return.

"Ah, the casual, outdoor type," Jose said as if he understood completely. "Well, let's get started." He turned around and led Gloria and Malcolm toward the back of the store.

Before he knew it, Malcolm was positioned before a full-length mirror, where he watched the little man whip out an assembly line of measuring tapes. Malcolm stood as still as he could, but there was a level of indignity associated with a man roaming his hands in places too close to the family jewels.

Having all this done while standing before Gloria's attentive gaze had Malcolm's face burning with embarrassment.

"You know," Jose said, popping up from the floor like a jack-in-a-box. "I think I have just the suit for you. It's Armani, but it will do nicely, yes?"

"Sure. Whatever, man."

Jose nodded excitedly and disappeared into the back of the store.

Malcolm's gaze shifted to Gloria, who in turn just smiled prettily.

"Don't worry," she said. "Jose is the best in the business."

As if that was what was truly bothering him. Malcolm held his tongue. The sooner this was over the better.

"Here we are," Jose said, returning. "Try this one on."

Gloria stood and admired the tux. "Ooh. This is nice," she said, rubbing her hand over the material.

Jose handed the suit to Malcolm. "You can try it on in that dressing room right over there. I think there are a few others you should also try. I'll be right back."

Malcolm shrugged and turned toward the dressing room. When he opened the door, he stopped and turned around to find Gloria marching behind him. "Do you mind? I do know how to get dressed."

Her cheeks darkened into a deep burgundy. "Oh. Yes, yes. Of course. I wasn't thinking," she said, clearly embarrassed. "I'll just wait out here."

Shaking his head, Malcolm turned and entered the dressing room. He grumbled under his breath the whole time. "I need my head examined. How did I let her talk me into this?"

A few minutes later, he stood cocking his head this way and that, trying to judge whether or not he liked the suit.

"Well?" Gloria said. "How does it look?"

"It looks like a tux," he said.

"Come out here so I can take a look." He rolled his eyes, feeling like a kid shopping for back-to-school clothes with his mother. When Malcolm stepped out of the dressing room, Jose and Gloria stood side by side taking their measure of him.

"Turn around," Gloria ordered, sliding on her glasses.

Malcolm jumped when two sets of hands groped his backside.

"What we'll do is tighten it up right here," Jose said. "And let this part out a little bit."

"Hmm," Gloria responded. "I don't know. Maybe he should try on that Valentino," she suggested.

Another suit was thrust toward Malcolm with the instruction to "Try it on."

Malcolm drew a deep breath and marched back behind the dressing-room door. However, the twosome repeated their evaluation performance for the next fifteen suits and Malcolm's patience had neared its end.

"How does it look?" Gloria asked yet again.

Malcolm ignored the question like he'd done the last couple of times.

However, Gloria's patience must have been nearing its own end because the next thing he knew she'd barged into the dressing room to take a look for herself.

"Hey!" he barked.

"Hey, yourself," she said. "We've been here for almost three hours. Is it too much to ask for you to hustle it up a bit?"

Malcolm just gaped at her as she held up the next jacket and urged him to slide his arms through the sleeves. He did as he was told, and then quickly started buttoning and zipping his pants while she attacked the buttons on his vest and jacket.

"I think this is going to be the one," she said.

Malcolm caught a whiff of her hair's fragrance and liked how it mingled with the floral scent of her skin. She smelled wonderful—more than wonderful, actually. Leaning forward to get a better whiff, Malcolm ignored her rambling about how the cut of this accentuated this, that and the other. He was too busy being seduced.

By the time she glanced up at him, their faces were just inches apart—their breaths warming each other's faces. Malcolm kissed her.

Chapter 7

Gloria had never swooned in her life.

But the moment Malcolm's lips brushed hers, she was lost. When his tongue swept inside her mouth, her brain emptied of all thought, her breasts perked against their lacy confinements while an ache throbbed at her core. Her body reacted on its own accord. Her hands slid over his shoulders, around his neck, and then pulled him closer.

Nothing had ever tasted so good.

She moaned against his lips and opened her mouth wider so he could get a sample of her, too. Gloria loved the feel of his strong hands caressing her back and then settling against her round butt. As he gave it a light squeeze, she moaned again and pressed her body closer.

It wasn't until the sound of Jose clearing his throat did reality seep into Malcolm's and Gloria's brains. They leaped apart, their shock mirroring each other's.

"What in the hell was that about?" she snapped, running her hands through her hair and trying to pull herself together.

"You tell me," he said, frowning.

"How should I know? You kissed me!"

"And you kissed me back," he challenged.

She stammered and sputtered. "Then it was temporary insanity," she said.

He laughed. "Temporary, huh?"

Her eyes narrowed. "I can promise you one thing, it will never happen again." Gloria's stomach jerked in response at that declaration. She would very much like to kiss him again. At this moment if, in fact, she could somehow render Mr. Hernandez mute and have him disappear for a few more minutes.

Instead of responding with another rude or sarcastic wisecrack, Malcolm just lowered his eyes to her kiss-bruised lips, as if her words were taken as a challenge of some sort.

Jose cleared his throat. "Does this mean you've decided on the suit?"

* * *

After another ride in Gloria's flying death trap, Malcolm arrived back at his office and climbed into the safety of his own vehicle. But he could only shake his head as he watched her speed out of the parking lot as if she had the devil himself nipping at her heels. He didn't blame her, really. That kiss had shaken him up, too.

What disturbed him the most was that he could still taste her: mint with a hint of citrus. Her tongue had been smooth as silk, while her moans were like the sweetest music he'd ever heard. Malcolm closed his eyes and relived the kiss again inside his head. All too soon, he blinked out of his trance and started the car.

"Get a grip," he coached himself, and finally headed out of the parking lot.

Despite his desire to head home, order pizza and see if there was a game on somewhere in the western hemisphere, Malcolm remembered his promise to his mother and instead headed out to the family estate.

During the whole drive, Malcolm tried to prepare himself for what he might find. He feared anything that would look or sound as if his mother was falling apart. Once he was within two miles of his old childhood home, the devil sitting on his right shoulder whispered a thousand reasons why he should delay his visit, but what they all boiled down to was guilt and shame.

How many times had his mother asked him to end the silly feud between him and his father? How many times had he dug in his heels and adamantly refused? A sad chuckle tumbled from his lips while the backs of his eyes burned. His mother and Gloria were right; he and his father were both stubborn.

The whole trouble started three years ago when thousands of Katrina evacuees poured into the Houston area and immediately caused a strain on Houston government services. Initially the city was more than willing to play the role of the good neighbor and accepted the evacuees with open arms. But then Texas had its own problem with citizens who also became evacuees when Hurricane Rita poached its shores a short time later.

The scramble for congressional money began and ended with Malcolm and his father on opposite sides of the table on exactly how to help the poor and growing homeless. Everyone promised to help, including Congressman Braddock, but once the media's cameras turned off, so did the money.

Then the fighting began. And it had been on ever since.

Malcolm pulled up to the family estate's security

gate, entered his code and waited for the tall wrought-iron gate to creep open.

Whatever dread and melancholy Malcolm feared was quickly forgotten the moment he crossed the threshold of his family's sprawling Tudor mansion. Instead, a smile curved his face at the smell of homemade apple pie, made by their housekeeper, Sarona. His favorite.

Since he hadn't called ahead, there was no one in the foyer to greet him, so he decided to let his nose lead him toward the kitchen, where he found two pies cooling on the counter and pot roast on the stove. His stomach let loose a ferocious growl and he nearly hurt himself scrambling to find a plate and silverware.

"What on earth is—"

Malcolm, sitting on a stool in front of one of the long kitchen counters, froze with his fork poised above his plate of stolen food when Sarona strolled into the kitchen.

For a brief moment her warm brown eyes lit up at the sight of him; however, in the next second, they narrowed into thin slits while her finger jutted forward and began to wag. "I should have known you'd sneak into my pots when my back was turned."

Malcolm smiled and gave his most woeful puppy-dog eyes at the petite older woman. "You know I can't resist your cooking, Sarona."

"You better not have touched my pies," she warned, turning and finding them unharmed on the counter. She sighed in relief.

"Those are next on my hit list," he promised, shoveling in his first bite of pot roast.

"Sarona, where—" Shondra stopped and allowed the kitchen door to swing closed when her gaze landed on her older brother. Instead of lighting up like their lovable housekeeper, she crossed her arms and speared him with a dirty look. "Well, look who's finally found his way home."

Malcolm drew a deep breath. "Evening, Shawnie."

"Evening? Is that all you have to say?"

"I meant to call you back." His set his fork down.

She grunted. "I don't know what the hell has gotten into you lately, but—"

"Shondra?" Their mother's voice floated into the kitchen and cut off Shondra's stream of obscenities before they really got started. "Who are you talking to in there?" Evelyn glided into the kitchen and gasped happily when she spotted Malcolm. "You made it," she exclaimed, rushing to wrap her arms around her frequently absent son. "I told your sister you wouldn't break a promise."

"Of course I wouldn't," he said, accepting her quick pecks on his cheeks. He took a good look at his mother to see how she was holding up. Her smile was luminous, but the uncharacteristic bags under her eyes and the round hunch of her shoulders told another story. She seemed smaller to him, weaker. He wished like hell there was something he could do to take away the pain she was feeling.

His selfishness in the past week really hit him and he realized right then and there that he needed to step up and be the man his father had always taught him to be. "I'm sorry, Mama. I should have been here for you this week."

From the corner of his eyes, Malcolm saw his sister's defensive stance slacken as if she was weighing whether to accept his apology as well.

His mother smiled and shook her head. "There's no need for you to apologize. I know you've been dealing with a lot. Regret is a very heavy burden, baby." She patted his cheek. "But it's time to lay it down," she said. "We're all going to have to try to find the strength to move on." Her arms wrapped back around his shoulders. "Together."

The love that radiated from his mother overwhelmed him and annihilated the weak wall he'd constructed around his heart. He couldn't carry the guilt anymore. He should have made up with his father when he'd had the chance. He should have never stopped telling the man who'd been his childhood idol how much he loved him—and loved him still.

Malcolm wrapped his arms around his mother, and for the first time since the news of his father's death, he wept.

Chapter 8

Malcolm hated ties.

Since he wore them so infrequently now he could never remember how the damn things were put on. Inevitably they were always crooked, too loose or too tight. After the hundredth time wrangling with the damn thing, he was ready to toss in the towel. Hell, maybe it wasn't too late to cancel this evening.

Malcolm plopped down on the edge of his bed and glowered at his image in the mirror. "How did you let her talk you into attending this damn thing?"

The phone rang, forcing him back onto his feet

so he could pick up before the call was transferred to his crowded answering machine.

"Is this Mr. Braddock?" the caller asked.

Malcolm frowned at the phone. "It is. Who's calling?"

"Mr. Braddock, this is Arnold Norton with Royal Limousine Service. I'm just calling to inform you that your driver should be arriving within fifteen minutes."

"Driver?" he asked, perplexed.

"Yes. A Ms. Kingsley ordered our services for this evening. She instructed us to pick you up at precisely 7:30 p.m."

"Then I'll be ready," he promised, and disconnected the call. Still, he didn't understand why Gloria would hire a service when Joe Dennis was still in his family employ. At least he was fairly certain he was.

Of course, he had never gotten around to asking his father's private driver why he wasn't driving the night of his father's accident, but he did make a mental note to ask Joe about that in the coming week.

The black, sleek limo arrived promptly at 7:30 p.m., and to his surprise, Gloria was already inside, nestled in one of the seats and smiling up at him.

"Good evening," she said in a sweet, honeyed voice.

Gloria may have been a beauty in black, but she was a seductive siren in red.

Malcolm was speechless.

"Here. Let me fix your tie," she said, scooting her way toward him. "It's crooked."

Staring, he remained still while her nimble fingers corrected his sloppy work. Her usual earthy floral fragrance was replaced by a bold heady scent that heated his blood and stirred his body. One part in particular.

"Now, that's better," she said, easing back and admiring her work. "Perfect."

His brain told him to say thank you, but the garbled mess that tumbled from his lips didn't resemble anything in the English language.

Gloria frowned. "Come again?"

Malcolm cleared his throat and tried again. "Thank you," he finally managed to get out.

"You're welcome." She turned in her seat and reached for her small purse. "I brought a…um, prepared speech for tonight."

"A speech?" he said, blinking out of his stupor.

"Well, yes. Seeing that your father was supposed to give a speech…I thought that maybe you could do it." She removed a folded piece of paper. "It's primarily about the advances the center has made in the past year and it urges everyone to continue to pledge their support. Harmon, um, your father had already signed off on the speech, but I've made a few changes…given the circumstances." She handed Malcolm the speech. "Do you mind?"

Malcolm glanced down at the words scrolled across the page and shook his head. "No. I'm honored."

Gloria sighed in obvious relief. "I was afraid you wouldn't be."

"No. No. I don't mind." He paused, folded the speech and tucked it inside his suit. "I know I've been a little…much lately. I apologize."

She blinked, surprised by the apology. "I understand." Gloria laid her hand against his leg.

Another bolt of kinetic energy shot through them and both knew that the other had felt it. Both of them stared at her hand before slowly lifting their gazes until they locked onto each other. They remained frozen in that position before Gloria finally slid her hand back into her lap.

"Sorry," she mumbled.

"For what?" he asked, and then watched her face darken a few shades.

She didn't answer. Or couldn't.

Malcolm smiled, relishing a rare moment when Gloria Kingsley had nothing to say. When he continued to stare at her, she glanced back over at him.

"Is something wrong?"

"No," he said. "It's just…I don't think I told you how beautiful you look tonight."

Her face darkened into a rich burgundy. Her lashes lowered. "You didn't have to say that."

"No. I mean it. You're absolutely stunning."

Her golden eyes lifted and studied him for sincerity. She was apparently satisfied, because her face lit up once again. "Thank you."

"No. Thank you. You're going to be on my arm. Trust me when I say every man in the place is going to be green with envy."

The Texas Children's Cancer Center fund-raiser was being held at the St. Regis Hotel, and from the moment they glided into the ballroom, surprised and curious men of distinction surrounded them and offered their hands and condolences. After a few minutes, Judge Bruce Hanlon parted the crowd like Moses and the Red Sea.

"Ah, Malcolm. So good to see you," Judge Hanlon said, jutting his hand into Malcolm's while using his free one to pat him hard on the back. "I see you finally went out and bought a new tux," he whispered close to his ear.

Gloria snickered, letting him know that she'd overheard the judge.

"Well, you know," he said with a laugh, "I'm really not a dress-up kind of guy."

"Maybe it's time to change all of that. Maybe it's even time to think of a career change as well?"

Malcolm cocked his head. "I think you lost me."

Hanlon caught the attention of a passing waiter and then graciously handed Gloria and Malcolm flutes of champagne. "Come, now. Surely you've given some thought to running for your father's seat in Congress?"

Malcolm nearly coughed up his first sip of champagne.

"No, no. You have the wrong man." He chuckled.

Hanlon's gray brows stretched, his blue eyes danced. "I'm never wrong about such things, son. Frankly, I think you're the most logical choice. You and your father held most of the same ideals and beliefs. Why wouldn't you want to carry on his legacy?"

Finding the whole conversation ludicrous, Malcolm chuckled and shook his head. "I'm not a political man."

"Politics is just another form of public service," Ray Cayman assured him, butting into the conversation and taking over. "You're the poster child for public service." Cayman looped an arm around Malcolm's shoulders and began walking him around the room while Gloria kept pace behind them.

"I've been following your career for a while now," Cayman said.

Malcolm wasn't surprised. It was starting to sound like spying on him was everyone's favorite pastime.

"What you've been able to do with the Arc Foundation is nothing less than amazing. People love you. Trust you. Believe me when I say you're the right man for the job."

They stopped walking and again a crowd formed around them.

"Now, I'm not going to pressure you," Cayman said. "But I think this is something you should give serious consideration to. The governor should be announcing a special election soon. You'd get my vote."

Malcolm nodded, hoping it was enough to get him off the hook.

"At the very least, you should think about it."

"I'll do that."

Gloria chose that moment to place a hand on Malcolm's shoulder and direct his attention across the room. "There's Mr. Roark. We should go over and say hello."

He nodded his appreciation and then flashed Cayman and Hanlon an apologetic smile. "If you'll excuse us?" Malcolm offered Gloria his arm and then escorted her across the room. "I'd appreciate it if you'd jump in a little sooner next time."

"Why?" she asked. "I happen to agree with Senator Cayman and Judge Hanlon."

He scoffed. "Me—running for office?"

She shrugged. "Why not?"

Malcolm frowned and cast a suspicious look. Was this what she'd been up to all along? He chuckled again. They were all barking up the wrong tree.

"Evening, Mr. Roark," Gloria greeted him once when they approached his intimate circle.

"Ms. Kingsley," Roark exclaimed. "You came." His gaze shifted to Malcolm. "And you managed to do what I could not."

She laughed. "It wasn't easy."

"Malcolm." Roark extended his hand. "Had I known all it took was a beautiful woman to get you here, I would have sent over my lovely Gertrude to reel you in."

Roark's better half laughed and leaned into her husband's arms.

Malcolm and Gloria grinned at the attractive couple.

"Please accept our heartfelt condolences for your loss," Gertrude added with a genuine note of sympathy.

"Thank you," Malcolm said.

Before an uncomfortable cloud of silence was able to settle over their heads, Gloria excused them and led Malcolm to the mayor, then toward a couple of pro football players and then at last to a chart-topping pop diva and her rap mogul boyfriend. Malcolm admired the way Gloria expertly glided them around the room as if they were performing their own private dance. She was amazing with re-membering names, positions and even whose children were sick or getting ready to go to college.

For most of the evening, he did feel like a budding politician, shaking the right hands and smiling into the right faces. All that was missing were a few screaming babies and an interview with Anderson Cooper.

After an hour of smiling, shaking hands and ac-cepting condolences, the organizers of the event were ready to start the evening's program. Midway through dinner, Malcolm was introduced and went up to the podium and delivered the speech Gloria had written for him. The applause was deafening and brought a few burning tears to the back of Malcolm's eyes.

In his head, he could hear his father's voice reading the words on the printed page. He knew just when his father would pause or raise his voice for dramatic effect. The speech was just a small thing, but Hanlon's legacy speech refused to leave him.

The rest of the evening breezed by and had it

not been for his catching Gloria yawning every two minutes, he might not have noticed it was nearing midnight.

"We can go if you're tired."

She shook her head and protested; but when she opened her mouth, she yawned again. "Oh. I'm sorry," she gasped in embarrassment.

He just laughed. "Let's go, Sleeping Beauty." As he escorted her toward the door, he murmured their goodbyes to those they passed in their great escape.

"Seems like you had a good time," Gloria said as they waited for their limo.

"I admit it wasn't as bad as I thought it would it be. Thanks for convincing me to come out of my shell…and for the new tux."

She smiled up at him admiringly. "I always thought that you just needed a woman to polish you up a bit."

"Is that right?"

"Surely you didn't miss how all those women were flirting with you tonight."

"What makes you think that doesn't happen all the time?" he challenged.

Their limo pulled up.

"Does it?"

"Well. I don't want to brag," he said, dusting his shoulders off.

Gloria rolled her eyes as their driver hopped out and opened their door. "C'mon, Romeo. Let's get you home."

Chapter 9

It turned out that Malcolm was just as tired as his companion. While he and Gloria reviewed the evening, they took turns exchanging yawns in the middle of their sentences until they could do nothing but laugh at themselves.

Gloria had never enjoyed Malcolm's company more. Plus, she was growing to like the way his voice rumbled whenever he laughed or how his lips sloped whenever he remembered an embarrassing comment. None of that compared to how she felt each time he said her name. It could have been just her imagination, but she could swear his tone deepened into a caress when he addressed her.

She shook her head. Yeah. It had to be her imagination.

Regardless, she liked this version of Malcolm Braddock instead of his usual stiff and stoic persona. This man could win the hearts and minds of the people and continue the good work his father had started.

"Hey, why aren't we moving?" Malcolm asked suddenly. He turned and glanced out of the window.

"I don't know." She blinked sleepily. She hadn't even noticed that the vehicle had stopped.

Malcolm pressed the speakerphone and spoke directly to their driver. "Is there a problem?"

The driver lowered the glass shield separating the back compartment from the driver section. "Traffic. I'm guessing there's been a bad accident. We're in the middle of a gridlock."

Gloria perked up in instant concern. "I hope no one was hurt."

"As soon as the roads clear up I'll get you two home."

Malcolm and Gloria nodded their appreciation and the glass divider slid back in place.

"Guess we'll be camping out here tonight."

"Well, I'm beat," she confessed, stretching and

yawning. "I hope you don't mind my making myself comfortable."

"Not at all," he said as she kicked off her shoes and curled up in her seat. "I'm guessing you were a cat in your former life."

Gloria smiled. "My mother used to say the same thing," she admitted. "I could always squeeze myself into rather small spaces when I was younger."

He cocked his head and frowned. "Why is that?"

She shrugged as she laid her head against the leather seat. "Probably I was just trying to get away from my parents' yelling and screaming. Of course, that was a constant occurrence when they were still together."

Silence followed her admission, and when she fluttered her eyes open it was to see Malcolm staring down at her.

"You really did have it pretty rough growing up."

Gloria gave another listless shrug. "Others have had it worse. I'm just grateful they finally split. You know, some couples try to stick it out for the kids when in fact it just makes things bad for everyone involved."

"You sound bitter," he said.

"I'm not. Besides, the experience has made me what I am today. Strong and independent." She lifted her chin. "I wouldn't change a thing."

That adorable slope to his lips returned. "Nor would I."

She smiled despite her eyelids drooping. "So you think the Arc Foundation will be doing more work with the center in the future?"

"Definitely," he said, and then started tossing out ideas on how to raise awareness for all that the foundation was doing for the community.

Gloria started drifting; the sound of Malcolm's voice was like a warm blanket. The next time she managed to open her eyes, she was enveloped in his masculine scent and nestled against his hard chest. Embarrassed, she started to pull away, but Malcolm's arm tightened around her in silent possession despite his being fast asleep.

She sighed while a smile of contentment curved her lips. Yet in the next second her eyes lowered again. She might have been mistaken, but for a split second she thought she felt his lips press against her forehead. She quickly dismissed the idea before drifting off to dreamland.

Malcolm awaited her there, too. Handsome and gallant in his new tuxedo, he offered her his hand for a dance. Gloria accepted it with a smile and glided effortlessly into his arms. This time, she wasn't wearing her red dress but instead a beautiful white gown that could have been a wedding dress.

Malcolm's approving smile lit up the room as he prepared to lead in their first dance. Love glowed in his eyes, and she could feel the powerful emotion radiate through her. As they floated around the room, Gloria had never been so happy.

Magically, the faceless crowd and ballroom faded, and then by magic it was replaced by a luxurious bedroom where an obscenely large bed encased in red-and-white silk stood prominently in the center of the room.

"Oh, Malcolm. It's beautiful," she said, spinning around in the room.

He only smiled and moved in close.

Gloria peeled off his jacket and the tiny buttons on his vest disappeared when she brushed her hands against them. Just the sight of his toffee-colored skin weakened Gloria's knees. His broad chest wasn't monopolized by muscles, yet it was hard as steel.

Malcolm's hand drifted across the back of her gown and it fell from her body like water.

The first touch of his hand cupping her firm breasts sent shock waves of pleasure throughout her body. When his pillow-soft lips captured a kiss, her soul stirred. Yet, it was the taste of him that intoxicated her and emptied her mind of all rational thought. Their tongues mated in an erotic dance that caused Gloria's body to awaken in ways it never had before.

Gloria returned the kiss with enough fever and emotion to cause Malcolm to moan in response. A victorious smile ghosted her lips at the feel of his sex pressed against her, making it clear once and for all just how much he wanted her. In answer, she lowered her hand and caressed his erection until he panted her name.

"Oh, Gloria," he said, nibbling on her ear. "You feel so good."

Hell, he didn't feel so bad himself, she thought— vaguely aware of how real this *dream* felt. Malcolm's strong and nimble hands were everywhere.

Her back.

Her butt.

Sliding in between her legs.

She shivered and the ache where her thighs met intensified. She needed relief—now.

Lolling her head back, Gloria gave Malcolm access to her long neck, her throat and collarbone. What she was experiencing paled in comparison when his hot mouth settled over a hard jutted nipple. His gentle suckling had a direct link to the throb pulsing in between her legs. Each caress of his tongue on her breast was like a long stroke against her clit.

That was until his fingers slid inside of her and tears of joy leaked from her eyes.

"Oh, God. You're so wet," he moaned. His

fingers worked inside of her as if she was a human slip-and-slide.

Gloria's hips thrust against his hand and pleasure rippled throughout her body and heated her blood.

"That's it. Come for me, baby," Malcolm coached.

She nodded, her hips picking up speed, rocketing her into the heavens. With no time to prepare, Gloria's orgasm exploded and caused fantasy and reality to splinter. She woke suddenly. Alarmed to find herself in the back of a limo, sitting atop Malcolm's lap with his hand planted between her legs and her breast spilling from his mouth.

Chapter 10

Gloria shot off Malcolm's lap like a rocket and scrambled to the other side of the limo, pulling and tugging her dress down.

A stunned Malcolm stared at her wide-eyed and confused. "That wasn't exactly the reaction I was hoping for," he mumbled.

"Did we just…please tell me we didn't," she pleaded.

"Well, you did. I didn't," he said with a devilish grin. "I was sort of hoping I'd be next." Malcolm watched as horror blanketed Gloria's face. "Or not."

Her reaction killed his hard-on. "Did I miss something here?" he asked.

"I didn't think we were...I thought I was... dreaming."

He lifted a dubious brow. "Dream of me often, do you?"

"Never!"

His rumbling laughter now irritated her. "Methinks thou protest too loud...and too quickly."

She turned away from him and scrambled for her shoes.

"If it makes you feel any better, I thought I was dreaming, too...until you started fondling me."

"What? I did no such thing!"

He shrugged his shoulders as if he hated to be the bearer of bad news. Gloria suddenly remembered stroking his erection and moaned pitifully into the cup of her hand.

"Actually, I thought it was a nice way to wake a man up," he said, hoping to relax her a bit, but saw his friendly banter had the opposite effect. "Look, I'm sorry," he said, backpedaling. "I thought this whole thing was consensual."

Gloria stammered and stuttered but failed to string together a cohesive sentence. To complete her horror, the limo driver announced over the speakerphone, "We're here."

"Ohmigod! Do you think he saw us?"

"I don't know," Malcolm answered truthfully. "Do you want me to ask him?"

"Don't you dare!" She glanced around and grabbed her purse before the driver opened the back door.

Malcolm leaned over and touched her dress strap.

Gloria jumped and popped him on the hand. "Will you stop?"

Malcolm snatched his hand back. "I was just going to fix your dress before you flash the driver your lovely lady lumps."

Gloria glanced down and saw that one of her breasts was prominently exposed. "Damn it." She dropped her purse and quickly poured herself back into her dress.

The back door opened and Gloria launched out the backseat as fast as she could.

Malcolm chuckled and climbed out of his own seat. "Wait here," he told the driver, and rushed after Gloria.

"What are you doing?" she asked when he caught up to her.

"I'm walking you to your door."

"That's not necessary," she said, reaching the door of her apartment building.

"I know it's not necessary, but it is the gentle-manly thing to do." Of course, he made no mention that what had transpired in the back of the limo was missing on the list of gentlemanly behavior, but now was not the time to split hairs.

"Really, Malcolm. You don't have to do this." She continued her mad dash toward the elevator bay.

Malcolm said nothing as he followed. When the elevator arrived, they spread out to opposite corners of the small compartment. Malcolm seized the opportunity to apologize again. "Look, Gloria."

"I really don't want to talk about this right now."

"But I don't want you to be angry—"

"I'm not angry," she snapped.

Malcolm's brows lifted in dubious silence.

Gloria sighed. "It's been a long night and…a strange and embarrassing ride home."

"I rather enjoyed the ride home."

She groaned. "Look, I don't want you to think that I do that sort of thing all the time…or even some of the time. I—I've never behaved like that and I'd rather just put the whole thing behind me."

"But what if—"

"Please."

A strained and awkward silence hung for a few long seconds. Finally, a bell chimed and the elevator doors slid open.

Once again, Gloria took off and Malcolm's long legs kept pace next to her. However, her great escape was delayed by her inability to get her keys out of her purse and into the door.

"Okay. You've walked me to my door, you can go now," she told him, wondering why she couldn't seem to get her key into the door. She glanced up at the number and cursed under her breath. "Damn it. Wrong door." She turned and walked one door down.

Malcolm chuckled. "Gloria, I think—"

"'Night, Malcolm." She unlocked her door and raced inside almost in the same motion.

"But—"

The door slammed in his face.

He dropped his head against the wooden partition and drew a deep breath. "I guess that means good night." For a moment he thought about knocking. This seemed like an odd place to leave things, but what choice did he have?

He lifted his head, stared at the door and then finally walked away.

Gloria closed her eyes and exhaled when she heard Malcolm move away from the door. Shame and embarrassment were too mild to describe what she felt. Mortified was more like it.

"How am I ever going to face him again?" she wondered wildly as she slid down to the floor and cupped her face. More than anything, she wanted Malcolm's respect, and in one evening she'd blown her chances of that by acting like a loose hoochie who hadn't been laid in a year.

Actually, it had been more like eighteen months—but he didn't need to know that.

She sighed and prayed for the earth to swallow her whole. Instead, her mind decided to replay what had transpired inside that limo. Did she truly come on to him first?

A small chuckle tumbled from her lips imagining herself making such bold moves. Despite what she said, the truth of the matter was it wasn't her first time dreaming about Malcolm. That phenomenon started the night they'd met. She'd been thrown off by his handsomeness and had only made some barb about his suit as a way to pretend that she'd been unaffected by him—unlike the other women in the room who were tripping over themselves, trying to get his attention.

Either he was blind or he was pretending, also.

In the past few years, the girlfriends that she'd known about never lasted for long. Either they couldn't take the long hours Malcolm dedicated to his charities or they never thought that the son of a wealthy congressman lived such a frugal lifestyle.

Gloria knew enough about Malcolm to know that

he didn't like pretense and would choose brains over beauty in a New York minute. She even knew that his one serious girlfriend from college was an unconventional beauty who was as thick as she was curvy. It had broken his heart when she moved to New York and married some über-rich studio executive.

But that had been over a decade ago—surely, he was ready for love again.

"Wait," she said, lifting her head. "What am I saying?" she wondered. "Why in the hell should I care about his love life?"

Her love life paled in comparison—the operative word *love* being used loosely. She'd dated regularly throughout college but found that men usually were intimidated by her intelligence and/or her overzealous A-type personality.

Harmon had thought she and Malcolm would make a perfect pair. Could he have been right?

"No," she reprimanded herself, and tried to banish the thought; but then she remembered the feel of his breath drifting across her neck.

She shook the thought from her head and climbed onto her feet. "All I want is for him to run for his father's seat."

His mouth on her breasts.

She shook her head again. "It's just business."

His hands sliding in between her legs.

"Business!" She stomped her foot and became acutely aware that she was acting a little crazy. She chuckled as she headed to the bathroom. A hot shower would be just the thing she needed to purge Malcolm Braddock from her mind.

It worked.

Right up to the point when she climbed into bed, turned off the lights and drifted off where once again Malcolm awaited her.

Malcolm tossed and turned throughout the night. Nothing he did could get the image of Gloria out of his mind. The woman who had awakened him and stirred his passion in the back of that limo had been the polar opposite of the businesslike, straitlaced executive assistant who'd always run his father's office like a five-star navy general.

The woman who'd writhed on his lap and cried out his name in the most sensual, erotic voice he'd ever heard was like no fantasy nymph he'd ever met before. And one he wished to see again.

Of course, there was just one catch—Gloria Kingsley apparently had no plans of letting him ever see that side of her again.

Malcolm grabbed a pillow and smashed it over his head in tormented frustration. Still, his body craved what it had been denied. How did he expect to sleep when all he could think about was how delicious she'd tasted?

In the next moment, Malcolm climbed out of bed and paced around his dark bedroom while he tried to make sense out of what he was feeling. By 2:00 a.m. he contemplated driving back over to Gloria's place and banging down the door. However, he'd run the chance of her either calling the cops or the good folks down at the local mental institution.

Sound reason convinced him not to chance it.

What if he called? Malcolm's gaze slid to the cordless phone on the nightstand next to his bed. He calculated the odds of her answering the phone. And if she did answer the phone—what should he say?

"Hey, can I come over so we can finish what we started?" He groaned at the notion. That would get him a fast introduction to Mr. Dial Tone.

No. He would need charm and finesse if he ever hoped to meet that uninhibited seductress again. And he *wanted* to meet her again.

Badly.

By 3:00 a.m. Malcolm found himself in the living room and rummaging through those old campaign tapes until he found, played and froze the images of Gloria.

This time when he studied her face, it was as if

he was seeing her for the first time. True, he'd always seen her beauty, but now he noted other things: the spark in her eyes that reflected curiosity and adventure, the firm line of her jaw that radiated strength and determination.

As Malcolm stared at Gloria's profile, his blood stirred once again and he remembered the sweet taste of her puckered nipples and how silky and hard her clit felt against his hand.

His growing erection pulsed and throbbed against his leg until he eased a hand down the front of his black boxers in order to get some release. The moment he wrapped his hand around his lengthy hard-on, he sucked in a sharp breath and groaned out her name.

Gloria tossed and turned against her bed's satin sheets. Her hand was planted deep between her legs while she recalled in vivid detail how Malcolm had lapped hungrily at her breasts—every other stroke she felt the soft graze of his teeth against her sensitive nipples.

Her breathing grew choppy while she made lazy figure-eight strokes along her swollen clit while her other hand squeezed and pinched her breasts.

Finding a good rhythm, Malcolm allowed his eyelids to lower while his mind transported him back to the limo. Instead of his hand, he imagined that he had penetrated her hot, tight body and her rocking hips were stealing a part of his soul.

With each pounding thrust, Malcolm ground his teeth together in hopes to prolong their coupling. Yet it was impossible. Gloria's body grew tighter as she rushed toward her building crescendo, forcing Malcolm's breathing to morph into a chaotic chug.

Gloria's body was on fire. So close to her orgasm, she'd locked her knees together, but her hand continued to stroke and caress. Her blood was close to boiling when she began to quiver and shake. Her gasps heightened its pitch. Malcolm's name tumbled from her lips repeatedly. Perspiration beaded across her brow as she now entered the realm of delirium.

The next imaginary stroke of Malcolm's cock detonated Gloria's orgasm. She tossed among the pillows as a strangled cry of release filled her bedroom.

Growling, Malcolm's orgasm sped toward him with the power and force of a locomotive and then collided and shattered his soul into a million pieces. When he opened his eyes to see Gloria's smiling face still frozen on the screen he realized that he was far from being satisfied.

And wondered if he ever would be.

Chapter 11

Gloria woke the next day with a renewed determination to put last night's embarrassing episode behind her. Today, what was left of the Harmon Braddock staff would learn when the governor would announce the date of the special election for the vacant Twenty-ninth District seat in Congress.

The clock was ticking for her to convince Malcolm to run. A feat complicated now that she was too embarrassed by her behavior last night to face him again.

Selecting a no-nonsense black suit and black boxed pumps, with her hair pulled and pinned into a tightly coiled bun, Gloria hoped the outfit would help erase the image of the wanton woman from last night.

With any luck, Malcolm would help her pretend that the whole episode never happened.

All hopes of that were dashed the moment she entered her office and found it filled with red roses.

"Looks like somebody has an admirer," Mabel sang out, coming up behind Gloria. "Sorry for last night. You were right."

"You read the card?" Gloria snapped.

Mabel shrugged. "We were dying with curiosity. We didn't think you ever dated."

"We?"

Amelia Blake poked her head into the office and waved. "Curiosity usually kills the cat, but we were willing to take that chance."

Gloria drew a deep breath and silently counted to ten.

"There's just one thing," Mabel said, watching her boss stomp over to her desk. "Didn't you go to that cancer center fund-raiser with Malcolm Braddock last night?"

Gloria hoped against hope that her face didn't look as inflamed as it felt, but judging by the women's immediate squeals, it was clear it was a lost cause.

"The roses are from him, aren't they?" Mabel

asked, rushing up to Gloria and grabbing her arm as if they were suddenly new best friends. "We want all the juicy details."

Gloria smiled, and then gently but firmly pried her hand from Mabel's grasp. "There's nothing to tell," she lied, and then eased behind her desk.

The women's faces fell.

"You're joking, right?" Amelia said, crossing her arms in preparation to stare Gloria down. "Honey, a man doesn't clean a florist out of their stock of roses unless *he* either did something wrong or *you* did something right."

"*Very* right," Mabel clarified.

Gloria's laughter was absent of humor, and her gaze darted everywhere but toward the two sets of eyes trained on her. "C'mon, now. You know Malcolm and I usually rub each other the wrong way."

"Please," Amelia said, rolling her eyes and making herself comfortable on the edge of Gloria's desk. "All that fake arguing you two do have never fooled anybody."

"Tell me about it," Mabel grumbled in agreement.

Amelia went on, "Whenever you two are in the same room together we have to turn up the air conditioner in order to cool the place down."

Gloria's eyes widened as she shook her head. "You two are just playing devil's advocates."

Mabel's lips sloped into a half smile. "Are you saying that these roses *aren't* from Malcolm?"

Gloria scowled at being backed into a corner.

"Aha!" The women shouted in unison and jumped to their feet. "We knew it. We knew it."

Gloria moaned as the women rocketed behind her desk and rolled her chair back so they could get up close and personal.

Mabel was first to get her question out. "Did y'all do the do or did you just tease him a bit?"

Amelia popped Mabel on the shoulder. "Of course she just teased him. Gloria isn't the type to just give up her goodies on the first date."

Gloria shrank in her seat in an attempt to become invisible.

"Please." Mabel turned to argue with Amelia. "When was the last time the girl has even gone out on a date? A girl can only suppress those urges for so long." She glanced back at Gloria. "Am I right? You didn't break him, did you? The man is still in one piece, right?"

Mabel now popped Amelia's shoulder. "Look, now you've stunned the girl speechless. Everyone knows Gloria is a *good* girl. Isn't that right?" She eyed Gloria for confirmation.

Gloria bumped her gums but words eluded her.

Blessedly, the phone rang and she jumped to answer it. "Hello."

Amelia and Mabel continued arguing while Gloria tried to discern the voice on the other line.

"Hello," she repeated.

"It wasn't an accident," said a strange and rushed whisper.

"What?" Gloria frowned and glanced up at the caller ID screen to read Unknown Number. "What wasn't an accident?"

Click.

A second later an automatic recording instructed, "If you'd like to make a call, please hang up and dial your number again."

"Humph. That was weird," Gloria said.

"At the very least we know that you kissed him," Mabel said, determined to get *something* out of Gloria.

"Ladies, do you mind?" Gloria said, reaching the end of her patience. "This is still a place of business and I have a ton of work to do."

Mabel looked outraged. "What—you're just going to leave us hanging?"

Amelia shook her head and laughed. "I told you we weren't going to get anything out of her. When it comes to gossip, honey-child's lips are sealed tighter than Fort Knox."

"I'm thinking that's what makes her such an exceptional executive assistant," a deep baritone said, silencing the women.

All eyes turned to see Senator Ray Cayman filling the open doorway.

"Good morning, ladies," he greeted them, tilting his groomed salt-and-pepper head toward them. "I hope I'm not interrupting anything important."

"Oh, no," Amelia said with a quick smile, and then elbowed Mabel to signal it was time to make their exit.

"Hello, Senator," Mabel said, practically mooning over the handsome septuagenarian. "Can I get you anything to drink? Coffee—tea?"

"No. I'm fine. Thank you."

Mabel bobbed her head, but it wasn't until Amelia gave her a quick shove did she think to leave the office. "All right, then. I guess we'll just leave you two alone."

Still smiling, Cayman nodded and then waited.

When the women finally made their exit, Gloria sighed in relief. "I'm completely in your debt," she said, chuckling.

Cayman glanced around the office. "I think you have every rose in the state of Texas in here."

She laughed. "I think you might be right."

"Boyfriend?"

So much for thinking she had escaped inquiring minds. "Um. Not exactly."

An Important Message from the Publisher

Dear Reader,

Because you've chosen to read one of our fine novels, I'd like to say "thank you"! And, as a special way to say thank you, I'm offering to send you two more Kimani Romance novels and two surprise gifts – absolutely FREE! These books will keep it real with true-to-life African American characters that turn up the heat and sizzle with passion.

Please enjoy the free books and gifts with our compliments...

Linda Gill

Publisher, Kimani Press

...off Seal and Place Inside...

We'd like to send you two free books to introduce you to our new line – Kimani™ Romance! These novels feature strong, sexy women, and African-American heroes that are charming, loving and true. Our authors fill each page with exceptional dialogue, exciting plot twists, and enough sizzling romance to keep you riveted until the very end!

KIMANI ROMANCE ... LOVE'S ULTIMATE DESTINATION

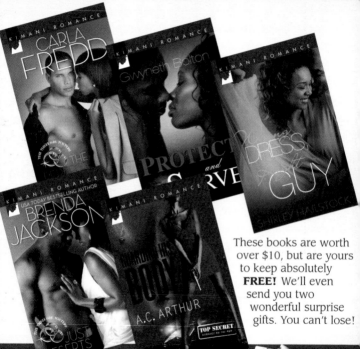

These books are worth over $10, but are yours to keep absolutely **FREE!** We'll even send you two wonderful surprise gifts. You can't lose!

2 Free Bonus Gifts!

THE EDITOR'S "THANK YOU"
FREE GIFTS INCLUDE:

Two NEW Kimani™ Romance Novels

Two exciting surprise gifts

YES! I have placed my Editor's "thank you" Free Gifts seal in the space provided at right. Please send me 2 FREE books, and my 2 FREE Mystery Gifts. I understand that I am under no obligation to purchase anything further, as explained on the back of this card.

PLACE
FREE GIFTS
SEAL
HERE

168 XDL ERR5   368 XDL ERSH

FIRST NAME

LAST NAME

ADDRESS

APT.#

CITY

STATE/PROV.

ZIP/POSTAL CODE

Thank You!

Please allow 4 to 6 weeks for delivery. Offer limited to one per household and not valid to current subscribers of Kimani Romance books. **Your Privacy** - Kimani Press is committed to protecting your privacy. Our Privacy Policy is available online at www.KimaniPress.com or upon request from the Reader Service. From time to time we make our lists of customers available to reputable third parties who may have a product or service of interest to you. If you would prefer for us not to share your name and address, please check here ☐. ® and ™ are trademarks owned and used by the trademark owner and/or its licensee. © 2008 Kimani Press.

DETACH AND MAIL CARD TODAY!

BUSINESS REPLY MAIL
FIRST-CLASS MAIL   PERMIT NO. 717   BUFFALO, NY

POSTAGE WILL BE PAID BY ADDRESSEE

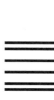

**THE READER SERVICE
3010 WALDEN AVE
PO BOX 1867
BUFFALO NY 14240-9952**

NO POSTAGE
NECESSARY
IF MAILED
IN THE
UNITED STATES

"Ah. I'm being nosy, aren't I?"

Gloria shrugged as she slid on her glasses. "Well…"

A long strained silence drifted between them.

"Was there something you needed, Senator?" she asked, noting the oddity of him just showing up unannounced.

"No. Well…" He paused. "It sure is strange without Harmon around," he said softly.

Gloria nodded sadly. She hadn't stopped noticing the large void Harmon left. Knowing how far back the senator and Harmon went, Gloria understood completely what he was going through.

Cayman stood as if he had more to say but didn't know how to go about saying it.

Gloria didn't know what to do, so she kept her eyes averted and braided her fingers while she waited. It'd always pained her to realize that when it came to these sorts of things, she was severely lacking. She had always dealt with grief and disappointment by keeping busy. "Worrying and tears are a complete waste of time," her mother had drilled into her, and it had become her personal decree.

As if noticing the silence, Cayman cleared his throat and offered her a weak smile. "You're probably wondering why I stopped by," he said, and moved to the vacant chair before her desk.

Gloria smiled.

"It's about last night," he offered, sitting down and adjusting his tie. "I wanted to feel you out about whether you thought Malcolm had given any serious thoughts about what we discussed last night."

Gloria's interest piqued. "About running for his father's seat in Congress?"

Cayman nodded. "I've talked with a few of my constituents and…" He met her gaze. "Can I be honest with you?"

Nodding, she leaned forward in her desk. "Everyone is practically salivating at the thought of Malcolm stepping in and continuing his father's work. People love the work he's been doing for the community. Hell, he fared much better than any of us after that Katrina nightmare. If we get his name on the ballot, he's a shoo-in."

Gloria hid her delight behind a well-cultivated poker face. "Has the governor announced when the special election will take place?"

"This morning. Four months from today," Cayman said. "So if we're going to do this, we need to make our own announcement soon."

She agreed but realized that she hadn't really made a dent in convincing Malcolm to pursue a career in politics. Truthfully, she wondered if she ever could. Even Harmon had failed in the endeavor. What made her think she could do it?

Cayman cocked his head. "Well, what do you think?"

She finally drew a deep breath and answered honestly. "Malcolm is his own man and driven by his own sense of right and wrong. While he may love working for change, he has a low tolerance for the whole political game."

Cayman nodded. "We all did—in the beginning. My question is do you think we can turn him around?"

She sighed and confessed, "I've been working on it."

This time, he smiled. "Harmon always said you operated two steps ahead of everyone else. I'm glad to hear we're on the same page." He stood and she did likewise. "There's a political fund-raiser next Wednesday hosted by Stewart Industries. Is there any chance of getting Malcolm to attend?"

She started to say that the country had a better chance of balancing the budget, when an idea hit.

"You're thinking," Cayman said, cocking his head. "What is it?"

Knock. Knock.

Gloria jumped as her eyes flew toward the door. Malcolm filled the space, wearing casual khakis and a loose-fitting T. In his hands was a lush bundle of red roses.

"Looks like there are more roses in the state, after all," Cayman joked as he approached Malcolm with his hand extended. "I'm almost afraid to ask what you did wrong, son."

Malcolm's gaze slid toward Gloria, who quickly glanced away.

"Well, hopefully it's something I can fix," he answered, accepting Cayman's handshake. "If you two are busy, I can come back later."

"No, no," Gloria answered, her friendly smile shaky at best. "The senator was just trying to convince me to go to a *party* but I was telling him as much as I wanted to go, I didn't have an escort." She tossed out the risky bait and then held her breath.

Cayman glanced over his shoulder at her.

"Well, if you really want to go," Malcolm said, "I wouldn't mind taking you. When is it?"

Gloria beamed despite having used Malcolm's guilt from last night to her advantage. "Wednesday night. You're sure you don't mind?"

"No." Malcolm's smile broadened. "I'd love to take you."

Cayman chuckled. "Well, I guess that means roses really do work." He patted Malcolm on the shoulder. "I guess I'll see you two Wednesday night." He winked and shuffled past Malcolm at the door.

Gloria lowered back into her seat.

Malcolm edged closer to her desk. "I guess you know what this means?"

Confused for only a moment, Gloria laughed. "Yes. We are officially going on a date."

Chapter 12

Gloria may have been gorgeous in black, a sizzling siren in red, but she was positively breathtaking in blue. The moment she opened her apartment door, Malcolm was speechless. The dress, the shortest he'd ever seen her in, draped her curvy body like a second layer of skin and had a way of making her legs look like tall stacks of brown sugar.

"Looks like I'm not the only one who knows how to be on time," she joked, sliding on a sheer blue jacket and grabbing her matching clutch bag.

Malcolm stared.

"Well, I'm ready," she said with a careless shrug when it looked as if Malcolm was just going to stand there.

At last, he blinked and ended his trance. "You look magnificent," he said, knowing it was an understatement.

"What? This old thing?" She stepped out into the hall; but as she brushed past him, he caught sight of the price tag still attached to the back of her dress.

"Old thing, huh?" he said, barely containing his mirth as he grabbed the tag. "Forty-percent off is a pretty good deal."

"Oh!" She jumped, avoiding his gaze while her face darkened.

"Here. Let me take care of that for you," he offered, knowing from experience with his sister how to remove the tag without damaging the dress. "There you go. You're all set to break men's hearts."

Gloria glanced over her shoulder and looked up at him. "That's the first time I've been accused of that."

He leaned in close and allowed the trail of her heavenly scent to wrap around him. "Has anyone told you that you're not a very good liar?"

Her blush deepened. "Only you."

He smiled and offered his arm. "Now, where is this party?" he asked, wondering if he was a bit too casual for the evening in his all-black attire.

"Not far. The Lancaster Hotel," she said, and pretended not to notice his immediate frown while she led him toward the elevators.

"Fancy. Just what sort of party is this?"

"Oh, you know." She shrugged. "The usual." She tapped her foot as she mentally urged the elevators to hurry. There was a very strong possibility of making the *Guinness Book of World Records* for the shortest date.

Malcolm groaned as the elevator's bell dinged. "It's a political dinner, isn't it?"

"No," she answered, not quite meeting his gaze. "It's a political fund-raiser."

He scoffed. "And what, pray tell, is the difference?"

"Less food and more music," she said as if it was obvious, and stepped into the elevator.

He followed her. "I don't believe this. You tricked me."

"I did no such thing. You offered to take me out."

"Because you knew I would."

"What—I'm psychic now?" No way was she going to admit that she'd played on his guilt to get what she wanted. As far as she was concerned, he could never prove it.

"Did Cayman put you up to this?" Malcolm's voice thickened with rising irritation.

The bell chimed and the doors slid open.

Gloria quickly exited the small compartment in hopes to distance herself from his tight scrutiny.

Malcolm dogged her heels. "The answer is no," he said. "I'm not running for my father's seat, so you and your partner in crime can just forget it."

She kept walking as if she hadn't heard a thing he'd said.

"I'm not interested in all that political back-scratching, backpedaling and plain old back-stabbing required to just get someone to change a light bulb in Washington. If I see a problem, I get my hands dirty and fix it. It's less paperwork and no wasting of taxpayers' dollars."

"Sounds like a campaign slogan to me," she said flippantly. "Where's your car?"

"Are you listening to me?" He stopped in the center of the sidewalk and scowled at her. "I said I'm not running."

"That's nice. Where's the car?" she asked again.

Malcolm frowned. The one thing he could always count on with Gloria was a good argument. And now that he was all set and raring to go, she had pulled the rug out from under him by not participating.

What the hell?

"This way," he grumbled, and led her to his parked SUV a few feet down the sidewalk. His eyes

remained trained on her while he fidgeted with his
car keys and then opened the passenger door.

"Thanks," she said, and climbed inside.

Malcolm slammed the passenger door and
stormed his way to the driver's side.

During the drive to the Lancaster Hotel, Gloria
met Malcolm's growing sourness with an overwhelming stream of syrupy sweetness. One thing
she noted, despite his constant grumbling, that at no
time did Malcolm attempt to end the date. That at
least gave her hope.

"Ah, you two made it," Cayman greeted them
with a smile the moment they entered the hotel's
luxurious reception room.

"We wouldn't have missed this for the world,"
Gloria boasted above Malcolm's disgruntled grunt.
"Thanks for inviting us."

Cayman nodded but turned his attention toward
Malcolm. "There are a lot of folks here tonight that
want to meet you."

"Is that right?" Malcolm said in a lazy attempt
to cover his sarcasm.

It took everything Gloria had not to stomp on his
foot with her four-inch stilettos and order him to
snap out of it.

"Now, now. Don't shoot us down before you
hear us out," Cayman cut in expertly, and swung

his arm around Malcolm's shoulder in a half bear hug. "You did promise to think about this exceptional opportunity."

Was that what these people thought his father's death was—an exceptional opportunity? Malcolm's stomach turned. "You know, Senator, there really isn't much to think about. I'm not interested in taking my father's place."

Cayman laughed and shook his head. "Stubborn. Just like your father."

Malcolm caught Gloria's slight nod.

"No pressure," Cayman said. "If you decide to turn us down, another candidate has come to our attention. Clint Hardy. Perhaps you've heard of him?"

Gloria perked with interest. "Clint Hardy?"

Cayman's smile bloomed wider as he tossed a wink in Gloria's direction. "Should have known that you'd know who was on the political rise in this town."

Not only that, Gloria knew Clint from college. He was a star athlete when she was at Texas A&M University. Clint was as handsome as he was charming, and it didn't hurt that his father, Andrew Hardy, once held the same congressional seat before Harmon Braddock.

On paper, the Hardys' political profile was just as impressive as the Braddocks'—which made Clint a serious contender.

"Is he here tonight?" Gloria asked, immediately searching the crowd to spot him.

Malcolm frowned at Gloria's sudden keen interest.

"Sure is," Cayman said, directing her attention to the opposite end of the conference room.

Stepping forward to get a better look, Gloria finally spotted Clint holding court with a group of nodding businessmen and women and looking every bit like a trained and polished politician. Gloria was worried.

"Ah, I see Hardy has cast his spell on you, as well," Cayman guessed, misreading Gloria's expression. "He is a charming devil. I'll give him that much. Would you like an introduction?"

"That's not necessary," Gloria said. "We've met."

Malcolm's frown turned into a scowl. "And when was this?"

Gloria shrugged. "Too many years ago for it to be important," she said. "I doubt he even remembers my name."

Just then Clint glanced up and caught Gloria's eye. She watched as he mumbled his excuses to his surrounding audience and then headed their way.

Surprised, Gloria blinked and straightened her posture.

"Looks to me like he remembers you," Malcolm growled.

She glanced over her shoulder at Malcolm and noted his stony expression.

"Gloria Kingsley," Clint said when he invaded her personal circle. "I can't believe it's really you."

Gloria's smile widened while her cheeks darkened in a flattered blush. "Mr. Hardy. I didn't think that you'd remember me."

"It's Clint—and of course I remember you." His eyes assessed her from head to toe. "What red-blooded man could ever forget you?" Clint grabbed two flutes of champagne and politely handed her one. "Back in college, you had every boy drooling after you, but you would never pull your nose out of those books long enough to notice."

Gloria continued to blush prettily. "I'm sure that's a gross exaggeration," she said, stealing her first sip of champagne.

"Not at all." Clint shook his head and stepped back to appreciate her every curve. "Wow. You look stunning in that dress."

"What—this old thing?"

Malcolm grunted and then cleared his throat, successfully drawing Clint's attention to him.

"Malcolm Braddock." Clint extended his hand. "It's nice to finally meet you. I hear that you may be my competition."

Malcolm looked at Hardy's hand as if he'd rather amputate it than shake it.

As if sensing Malcolm's animosity, Clint withdrew his hand and slid it into his pants pocket. "So much for friendly competition, eh?" he joked.

"That depends on what we're competing over," Malcolm said, curling an arm around Gloria's waist and locking her beside him.

Hardy's brows shot upward as understanding dawned in his eyes. "My apologies," Clint said, taking a cautionary step backward. "I didn't know you two were an item."

"Neither did I," Cayman said with an equal note of surprise.

"We're not," Gloria said, prying herself free with an awkward smile. "We're just friends."

Hardy perked with renewed interest. "Oh."

"Very *good* friends," Malcolm clarified. His iron hook dragged her back to his side.

Annoyed, Gloria glanced up at Malcolm before asking Cayman and Hardy, "Could you excuse us? We'll be back in just a second." She maintained a smile as she took Malcolm's hand and pulled him away.

Malcolm followed but cast a departing warning toward Hardy.

"What in the hell was all that about?" she snapped the moment she found a private spot.

"What?" Malcolm shrugged.

"Oh, don't play stupid with me. What was all that 'very good friends' crap you were feeding them?"

"I thought we were friends."

"That wasn't how you made it seem," she accused. "You practically told the man to back off because I was your girlfriend or something."

"Or something?" Malcolm echoed. "Look, *Ms. Kingsley*. Where I come from you don't go out with one guy and then spend the evening flirting with another."

"What?"

"We are on a date—or did you forget?"

"C'mon, Malcolm. It's not a date-date."

"Oh, really?" He crossed his arms. "Are you finally admitting that you tricked me here so Cayman can try to turn me into his latest puppet?"

Gloria's mouth moved, but no words came out. He had successfully backed her into a corner and she had to figure out some way to maneuver out of it. "I didn't say that," she finally whispered. "But can you calm down the whole 'Me, Tarzan. You, Jane' routine you have going? It's embarrassing. We're on a date. I'm not your possession."

Before Malcolm could agree, Cayman found his

way over to the couple. "Is everything all right over here?" he asked.

Gloria and Malcolm turned on their fake political smiles.

"Yes, everything is fine," Gloria answered.

"Never better." Malcolm's arm snaked around Gloria's waist. He ignored how she stiffened in his embrace. Let her be uncomfortable. It would give her a good taste of what he was going through at this farce of a date.

Cayman nodded as if he bought the lie. "Good. Good." He led Malcolm and Gloria over to his group of constituents who wanted to meet Malcolm. For most of the evening, Malcolm felt as if he was on a *long* job interview. Inquiring minds wanted to know his position on things from health care, immigration and home security.

He couldn't tell whether they were trying to convince him to run for congress or president. Incidentally, no matter what his stance was on any given issue, Clint Hardy held an opposite position. In no time at all, what had started out as friendly conversation had turned into a political debate. More often than not, Malcolm's responses solicited applause while Hardy sounded more like a robot, spitting out answers that he'd obviously been trained to recite. His speeches lacked sincerity, and he tried to rely on his sparkling veneer of a smile than concern himself with the facts of any given issue.

When Hardy finally ran out of memorized quotes, he jokingly teased that they should save their vigor for the political trail. Malcolm then had the uncomfortable duty of informing the crowd that he hadn't decided to run for office.

A ripple of disappointed moans followed his announcement.

"Well, Ms. Kingsley," Hardy said, taking her hand. "If I do take office, I hope you'll be staying on board to whip me into shape. I'll need a good executive assistant and I hear you're one of the best." He leaned forward and kissed her hand.

"I'll keep that in mind," Gloria said.

Hardy winked and then gave a curt nod toward Malcolm before strolling off.

"Tell me there's no way you'd actually work for that clown," Malcolm sneered.

"I learned a long time ago to never say never. Maybe you should take that advice, as well."

Malcolm's scowl returned in full force, but Gloria pretended not to notice.

"C'mon, Malcolm. You're a natural. You just went toe to toe with Hardy without so much as breaking a sweat. The crowd loved you."

Malcolm remained indifferent. "It's easy to

debate someone who doesn't even know the facts."

Gloria shook her head. "Has anyone ever told you how stubborn you are?"

A corner of Malcolm's lips curled. "It's been mentioned a time or two."

Throughout the night Malcolm smiled into more faces and shook hands with nearly everyone in attendance and everyone repeated the same phrase, "You should run for office."

When it all became too much, Malcolm decided to step out onto the hotel's veranda to get some much-needed air. The minute he stepped outside, he drew in a deep breath and tried to clear his mind. It took a few breaths to eliminate some of the tension coiled in his body. It was a starless night, he noted. A faint breeze barely stirred the air.

Why was he still there? If he truly wanted, he could have left hours ago. He thought about it for a moment. Maybe he wasn't turned off by the idea of running for his father's seat—especially now knowing an idiot like Hardy stood a good chance of winning the vacancy. Such a catastrophe would set Houston back twenty years.

Malcolm shook his head, mentally replaying the entire evening.

"It's a hard decision, isn't it?"

Malcolm turned to see Cayman gracing the doorway. "Do you have a homing device planted on me or something?"

Cayman laughed. "No. Nothing that serious. I just came out for a little fresh air. Looks like you beat me to it." He stepped out onto the veranda and offered Malcolm a cigar. "Smoke?"

"No. I never touch the stuff."

Cayman nodded and chewed off the tip. "I could never get your father to touch these things, either." After he'd lit up, he stared up at the sky. "You know, I've had the great pleasure of watching you grow up over the years," Cayman began. "Your father and I go way back."

Malcolm nodded, not really up for another speech about how great his old man was.

"I can't tell you the number of times your father worried about his kids, worried whether he was setting a good example or leaving a legacy that you guys could be proud of. I always assured him that he was worrying for nothing." He glanced over at Malcolm. "Maybe I was wrong?"

Malcolm ground his teeth together.

"In the end, every man hopes and prays that he's done enough to make the next generation proud. And we fear that our mistakes could erase the good we've done. I hope that hasn't happened with you."

"No offense, Senator, but you don't know me at all."

Cayman's smile curved around his cigar. "That could be a subject of great debate."

Malcolm's brows inched higher at the older man's overflowing confidence.

"For example, you think that following your father's footsteps into politics would mean that you've sold out. You don't like people looking at you and only seeing your father. You're your own man, right? You have your own way of seeing things—doing things."

Despite keeping his face neutral, Malcolm wondered when he'd become so transparent.

Cayman chuckled. "You're not the only one who's had to fight his way out of his father's shadow. I'm in my seventies and there are still people around who bring up 'Old Steamboat' Cayman, my father."

Malcolm relaxed his shoulders a bit and even smiled at the look of winsome nostalgia written across Cayman's face. "Was your father into politics?"

"Sort of. He was a sheriff. Tough on the outside—an old teddy bear on the inside. Still, he was a very popular fellow, and everywhere I went I was Old Steamboat's li'l boy. Still am." Cayman removed the cigar from his mouth and released a long stream of smoke into the air. "It was my father who had envisioned this life for me long before I had. I struggled and fought against it. I wanted to be the next Chuck Berry."

Malcolm laughed, unable to picture Cayman being a rock 'n' roller.

"Look, I'm not saying that parents are always right—but a lot of times they see something in us that we don't see in ourselves. Your father was a good man…but so are you. This route, this political route… You can do great things, probably more than you've ever dreamed of."

Malcolm turned away and cast his gaze back up to the starless sky.

"Think about it," Cayman said, and then disappeared from the veranda.

Once alone, Malcolm thought about the senator's words, and for the first time really considered whether he should run for his father's congressional seat.

Still undecided, he left the veranda in search for his "date." It was time to go. His gaze swept the conference room. Fake smiles and laughter were aplenty—the true face of politics as usual. Was this really what he wanted to be a part of?

Unable to locate Gloria, he quickly cased the room, asking attendants whether they had seen Gloria around. At last, the governor's wife pointed her out smiling and laughing up at Clint Hardy like a love-struck teenager.

He didn't remember plowing through the crowd, but when he reached Gloria's side, his hand clamped not too gently on her elbow.

"We're leaving."

Gloria's smile instantly melted off her face as her gaze fell to his possessive grip.

"If you like, I can take her home," Clint said. "We were having a nice conversation."

Malcolm's gaze sliced toward Hardy and effectively eliminated his fake smile, as well.

"No. That won't be necessary," Gloria said sweetly. "I am getting a little tired."

Malcolm nodded as if she'd given the right answer.

Gloria barely had time to say a proper goodbye before Malcolm dragged her toward the exit. Even while they waited for the valet to bring Malcolm's vehicle, Gloria read enough in Malcolm's face to know that he was an atomic bomb ready to detonate. She kept her mouth closed, biding her time until they were alone.

Only then would she declare war.

Chapter 13

"You have some nerve!" Gloria thundered the moment Malcolm shifted the SUV into Drive and peeled out of the hotel's parking lot. "You behaved like a complete Neanderthal in front of people who could make or break your political career."

"I don't have a political career."

"You're damn right you don't. Not after that little performance."

"Let me be clear," Malcolm sneered. "I'm not too interested in a political career, so you can stop plotting and planning with Cayman. So the next time you want to go to one these boring political fund-raisers, feel free to call up your new boyfriend Clint Hardy to take you."

"My boyfriend?" she bellowed and fixed her eyes on his stern profile. "Is that why you're throwing this little temper tantrum? You think I'm interested in him?"

Malcolm ground his teeth in silence.

"I wasn't flirting with him, if that's what you think. I was simply questioning him—"

"About a job," he jumped in. "I know."

"No. I was sizing up the competition," she defended. "No telling how many voters you turned off back there."

"I don't give a damn about what those people think," he spat. "I have my own plans, not that anyone's interested. And I don't like being manipulated." He jerked his gaze. "I would have thought that you'd have figured that out about me by now."

"You want to know what I've figure out?" She turned in her seat and challenged him. "That with all your bravado about being your own man and marching to your own beat, you're nothing but a scared little boy willing to throw away an opportunity of a lifetime just because you were mad at your old man."

"Goddamn it. How the hell can you of all people view my father's death as a *career opportunity?*

The man hasn't been in the ground two full weeks and everyone who claimed to love him can't wait to fill his shoes."

Malcolm took the next turn too fast and his tires squealed in protest.

"That's not how it is."

"Isn't it? Well, I happen to think his shoes were too big to fill—especially by me."

"Oh, don't give me that. You're just comfortable sitting on the sidelines, pointing and laughing at those who are truly trying to make a difference in this world. The truth of the matter is that you lack the guts to get in the game yourself. You don't like what's going on in politics, and if you think everyone is just a puppet or a puppet master, then jump in and do something about it. That's what Harmon was trying to do, whether or not he made mistakes. The point is that he *tried* to make a difference. What are you trying to do?"

Malcolm nearly swerved off the road. "Are you for real? Every day I get up, I try to make a difference in this world. I bust my butt trying to shelter the homeless, feed the hungry or get medical aid to the sick."

Gloria closed her eyes and drew a deep breath. "You're right. You and the Arc Foundation do some wonderful work—but let's face it. Those things are just Band-Aids on a larger problem. Real change comes from fighting for those same people through the system—homes, food and medical care should be a right, not an option in one of the richest countries in the world."

The fight seemed to shorten the drive back to Gloria's apartment, and before Malcolm had shifted the car into Park, she was out the SUV and storming toward her building.

No way Malcolm was letting her off the hook. "We're not finished," he barked, racing behind her.

"Oh, yes, we are," she snapped over her shoulder, and continued her trek toward the elevators. "I don't know why the hell I thought you had the balls—" she jetted into the elevator "—the guts to do what needs to be done. You don't give a damn about your father or the things that he cared about. He went to work every day with those political sharks and put his neck on the line. All you know—all you care to remember—is the few times he made mistakes. It must be nice to be *perfect,* Malcolm. How do you stand it to be on earth with us mere mortals?"

"I never claimed—"

"He was human, Malcolm. He made mistakes. Get over it!" They arrived at her floor and she jumped out as if she couldn't stand the sight of him another minute.

"I am over it," Malcolm charged, dogging her heels. "You're the one insisting I be something I'm not. When you look at me all you see is an opportunity to turn me into your idol. You don't see me. You just see my father."

Gloria jabbed her key into the lock. "Well, thank you for opening my eyes. Now, feel free to run home and hide in your quaint little apartment where you play poor little rich kid. Let real men with real balls fight the good fight. Men like Clint Hardy who know what they want and know how to go after it."

She'd finally done it, Gloria realized the moment Malcolm's face turned into stone and he slammed a fist against her door. It slammed open with a bang.

"How dare you," he seethed.

She stumbled in backward through the door while Malcolm stalked inside and then kicked the door closed behind him.

She backed away until she was pressed against the hall closet. He looked like he didn't know whether to hit her or throttle her.

"You're challenging my manhood now, is that it?" He pressed his chest against hers and gave her a good feel of his rock-hard erection. "Do you want to see how much of a man I really am?"

She honestly didn't know. Hell, she didn't think she could handle standing much longer.

"What's wrong, Gloria? Cat got your tongue?" He found another inch to move closer.

She closed her eyes and could swear she felt his erection pulsing in rhythm to his racing heartbeat.

"I asked you a question." Malcolm spoke softly while he wrapped a lock of her hair around his finger. "Do you think you can handle me? Or are you going to run away like you did last time?"

Her voice remained MIA. The fire in his eyes and the tautness of his broad chest pinned her to the closet. That absolutely turned her on.

She didn't wait for him to kiss her. She couldn't. In fact, there was no thinking involved. Just feelings—and what she felt was pure fire. Gloria's passion devoured him. His long winding moan sounded as if it came from a well deep inside of him.

With no space left between them, Gloria hiked up one leg and anchored it against his hip before bringing up the second and then locking her legs behind him. If she hadn't already been lost, the feel of Malcolm's iron-hard erection now pressed against her thin panties was enough to send her into no man's land.

She grabbed at his shirt and ripped it open with a strength she didn't know she possessed. There was no more denying that this was what she wanted. No more pretending that she couldn't stand him. For the first time in her life, she was going to toss caution to the wind and deal with the consequences later.

"Are you sure this is what you want?" Malcolm asked, dragging his lips away from hers to rasp against her ear. "I'm not going to be able to stop this time," he promised.

"Don't you dare stop," she growled back, and re-claimed his lips in a hungry kiss. Gloria was only vaguely aware of her dress inching up her body. It wasn't until their lips tore apart the second time that he pulled it over her head, getting rid of the thing. And frankly, she was too lust-drunk to give a damn.

"My God," he whispered, taking in the sight of her incredible body. Decked in a blue-and-black strapless bra, matching panties, garter belt, thigh-high stockings and high heels, she was ready for her own pinup poster. She looked like nothing he'd seen in fantasy or real life.

Malcolm lowered her feet back to the floor and found himself sinking to his knees before her. Her beautiful heart-shaped face was suffused with desire, and he felt an incredible pressure to please and satisfy her any way he could. On his knees, he was now eye level to her hips. He was unable to contain his desire to kiss her other set of lips.

Gloria's flat stomach quivered when his mouth peppered kisses around her belly button. Loving her response, Malcolm sank lower until he took the lacy fringe of her panties between his teeth and proceeded to pull them off her hips and down her smooth legs.

Slowly, she stepped out of the small material and then spread her legs a little wider as she watched him climb back onto his knees. This time he was eye level to her velvet V of black curls.

Once again, Malcolm was awestruck by her beautiful body. As if in a trance, he leaned forward and planted a kiss against her springy curls.

Gloria sighed, her legs visibly trembling.

He kissed her again. This time, his tongue glided inside her.

"Oh, God," she moaned, dropping her head back against the closet door.

She had stolen the words out of his mouth. Her body was sweeter than anything he'd ever tasted. His next kiss had his tongue sliding in between her thick lips, plunging deep and sapping up her body's juices as if they were the elixir of life.

Gloria lowered her hands to Malcolm's head— at first to pull him away because the pleasure was too intense, but once they reached their destination, she could do no more than massage and urge him on in his glorious feasting.

However, Malcolm needed no encouraging; he

continued to suck out her very soul with each gentle lapping of his tongue.

Her legs came up once again. This time she anchored them over his shoulders until she was literally sitting before his face while his hands cupped her ample bottom.

Suddenly, Gloria couldn't breathe. The pleasure was too much. She tried to squirm away but had nowhere to go. Her hand found the door to the closet just as her body shuddered in release and liquefied her every bone and muscle.

And still Malcolm continued to lap her up until she begged for mercy.

But she slipped sideways and the door slid open on its track. Gloria tumbled inside, dragging down coats and jackets on top of her.

At any other time, the couple would have laughed.

But the fire was too hot, the passion too intense for them to stop now.

Malcolm pulled and tugged out of his pants and got them off in record time.

At the first sight of Malcolm's incredibly rigid, toffee-colored erection, Gloria's mouth watered. She absolutely must have a taste of him.

Pulling herself out of the closet, she wrapped her hand around his beautiful thick work of art as if she was in awe. She leaned in close and drew him into her mouth, knowing instantly that she would forever remember his rich taste.

"Oh, Jesus." Malcolm exhaled as his straining flesh bobbed in and out of her mouth. For some reason he hadn't expected her to share his love for oral sex, and he certainly didn't expect her to bring him to the brink of madness so quickly.

In order to prolong the moment, he forced himself to pull her away and scramble for his condoms in his wallet.

After rolling one on, he eased Gloria onto her bed of fallen coats. She squirmed a bit when he pushed just the head of his sex inside her, giving her time to adjust to his girth. He took his time, inching his way into her hot passage and watching how the O shape of her mouth widened as he did so.

Once her slick body accepted his full length, he waited a few heartbeats until she rocked impatiently against him before he started moving languidly in slow torturous strokes.

He loved how high her sighs climbed and how she couldn't seem to stop saying his name. Nothing in his life had ever felt so right and so perfect.

He never wanted this night to end.

Malcolm teased her with long fluid strokes, taking his time to rotate his hips just so and hitting all her hot spots. So long, in fact, he counted her erupting with three body-quaking orgasms before he sought to get his own. He picked up the speed, grabbed hold of her long legs and used them as handlebars.

When he finally allowed himself to give into his own budding orgasm, he was thrusting hard and fast and had lifted her hips high off the floor. With one final stroke, Malcolm's orgasm raged through his body like a hurricane, and he collapsed on top of her.

They lay there, panting—half of their bodies inside the closet. They looked at each other, laughed, but waited for their second wind.

Minutes later, when they caught their breaths, Malcolm rained more kisses across her dewy brow while he freed her creamy brown breasts from their lacy confinements.

Just the sight of their perky ripeness made him hard again, but this time he asked, "Why don't we take the next round into the bedroom?"

Gloria smiled. "Great. I have a wonderful walk-in closet."

Chapter 14

Malcolm fell asleep with the sound of Gloria's orgasmic cries ringing in his ears. Never had he had a woman satisfy his every need. It blew his mind how Gloria's lush body anticipated his every move and would respond by meeting his every thrust with one of its own. Even now while his mind floated in a pool of euphoria, his body tingled as if alive for the first time.

He curled toward her, cupping her curvy frame in an intimate spoon position and brushing her shoulders and neck with butterfly kisses.

This was bliss.

This was heaven.

This was love.

Malcolm opened his eyes—startled by the dangerous direction of his thoughts. Love? Had that word really crossed his mind?

Still on his side, Malcolm propped up on his elbow and stared down at the sleeping woman beside him. Despite Gloria's loose curls spread around her head like a dark halo, and her full, kissable lips whispering his name, Malcolm felt the sharp kick of panic hit him squarely in the gut.

Love?

He shook his head as if it would somehow erase the notion, but it took root. When had all of this happened? And why now?

If ever he stood at a crossroads, it was now. Malcolm no longer recognized his own life, and it was all moving too fast for him to catch up— and now this.

Lying back down on the pillow, Malcolm gazed at the back of Gloria's head and twirled a few strands of her hair around his finger—loving how even that carved a smile on his troubled face. While the question of love swirled inside his head, more questions crept from the recesses of his mind: How did Gloria feel about him? Was she attracted to him or just the idea of transforming him into her former idol?

That last question shifted the pain from his gut to his chest. He lay there, motionless and overwhelmed.

By the time the first rays of morning filtered through the bedroom window, Malcolm was more confused than ever, but his body was slowly stirring to life.

Maybe it was time to go.

Gloria stirred, her ample bottom pushed against his returning erection.

He sighed and planted more kisses along her shoulder blade. Seconds later, Malcolm slid his arm over her round hips and then glided his hands up to cup her firm breasts. She had just the right amount: a handful.

She moaned and hiked her butt higher. Their little game continued until Gloria's light giggles floated on the air. "You're the best alarm clock a girl could have," she whispered.

Malcolm smiled into the crook of her neck and then inhaled her body's musky sweetness.

Eyes closed, Gloria loved the feel of Malcolm's hands massaging her breasts and his hard-on sliding between her legs, begging for entrance.

A part of her couldn't believe that last night or even this morning wasn't a dream. If she had her way, they would never leave this bed.

Malcolm's whisper-soft kisses moved up the

column of her neck before he settled on nibbling the lower earlobe.

As she felt Malcolm's knee nudge her legs open, a lazy smile ghosted around Gloria's lips as she complied to give him better access. Almost immediately his hand abandoned her breast to dive in between her legs. At the first stroke of his fingertips inside her, Gloria's breath rushed from her lungs.

"Ooh," she sighed as his fingers made lazy circles around her swelling clit. In no time, a glorious heat simmered in the center of her body and then gushed like a California geyser. Stars flashed from behind her closed eyelids.

One.

Two.

Three fingers dipped deep into the well of her honeypot to find her slick and ready. Gloria didn't care whether she looked too wanton or too brazen; she only wanted to satisfy the growing ache pulsing inside her. She rocked her hips against his large, thrusting hand and prayed that he would soon stop his teasing and give her what she really needed.

As if hearing her thoughts, Malcolm withdrew his hand for a few torturous seconds while he ripped open another condom packet. When he returned to their previous spoon position, he nuzzled her neck, lifted her leg and entered her fully and completely.

Malcolm rasped out Gloria's name each time he withdrew and sank into her. His heart thundered at the feel of her body contracting all around him, until one stroke sent her tumbling headlong into an orgasmic storm.

They cried out at the same time before their bodies curled into each other's—the bed linen clinging to their dewy bodies.

The last thought that drifted through Gloria's head before sleep claimed her was that this was the man she'd waited for all her life. All this time, he was right in front of her and she never knew.

Malcolm Braddock was a real man.

He was the one she could spend her whole life with.

He was honest to a fault, passionate and had just stolen the keys to her heart.

She felt a kiss to the back of her neck and fell asleep dreaming that this was the beginning of a beautiful relationship.

What she hadn't counted on was waking up to an empty bed.

Chapter 15

"Earth to Malcolm." Paula snapped her fingers.

Malcolm blinked, sat up and glanced around the conference room. A few coughs rippled around the large table while a few volunteers shook their heads in sympathetic concern. He'd heard the whispers of those thinking his quick return to work was a mistake—that his burying himself in work was fooling no one.

Maybe there was something to that. After all, it'd only been two weeks. Two weeks, his mind echoed. Was that all? It seemed he'd been battling this hole in his heart for a lifetime.

Paula frowned and stretched a supportive hand out to him. "Maybe you should sit this meeting out?"

"No, no. I'm fine." Malcolm cleared his throat and straightened in his chair. "You were just talking about…?"

"The Malawi Outreach program," she supplied. "We're waiting for you to update us on the details."

"Right. Right." Malcolm flashed an awkward smile to the ring of senior volunteers. He'd forgotten his pending five-week teaching program. "As many of you know, the Arc Foundation has decided to join forces with the World Camp Organization. They have spearheaded a successful program, working with thirty thousand children with one-hundred-and-fifty rural schools and street shelters in Malawi. They allow individuals to make a significant impact teaching HIV and AIDS education. The next session starts in September—a couple of weeks from now."

Paula bobbed her head and jumped in, "So far we have fifteen volunteers ready to go for the first session and ten signed up for late October." Her gaze slid back to Malcolm. "We have more than enough for the first session, so if you want to delay your trip…?"

Malcolm shook his head. He needed this trip to clear his head. "That's not necessary." He pulled on his smile. "I'm actually looking forward to going."

Paula's frown deepened, but before she could

question him further, he excused himself to go to the bathroom.

Kevin, the office manager, caught him just outside the men's room. "Mr. Braddock, I have an important call on line one for you."

Malcolm frowned. "Who is it?"

"It's Gloria Kingsley."

Malcolm's hackles stood at attention. He cleared his throat and said, "Tell her I'm in a meeting and I'll call her back."

"Yes, sir," Kevin said, his face flushed in embarrassment as he backed away.

"I'm sorry, but Mr. Braddock is in a meeting. He said he'd have to call you back."

Gloria's grip tightened on the phone as her jaw proceeded to grind her back teeth into powder. "Just have him call me at my office," she said, and then recited her number, though she suspected Malcolm knew it by heart. Returning the phone to its cradle, Gloria lowered her face into the palms of her hands as a way to stave off her burgeoning tears.

What the hell was going on? Why wasn't Malcolm taking her calls? She had called him more than once. She thought their passionate night meant something. At least a phone call.

After waking to an empty bed, Gloria had

stumbled into work more than three hours late. That act alone kicked the office's gossip grapevine into overdrive. Everyone knew she and Malcolm had attended Cayman's political fund-raiser last night. A few attendees from the office had also witnessed Malcolm's possessive behavior and how he'd literally dragged her out of there when he'd caught her chatting with Clint Hardy.

Compliments about her glowing skin and springy walk were a staged fishing expedition by the water-cooler crowd attempting to get the scoop on her resuscitated love life.

Love life. That was a laugh. She didn't know what was going on between her and Malcolm right now. She just hoped it wasn't a one-night stand. When she'd first awakened to an empty bed, she'd foolishly thought Malcolm was in the shower. Then she thought he was in the kitchen. By the time she'd finished exploring her apartment she struggled to face the harsh reality that he was gone. All that was missing from the pathetic scene was money left on the nightstand.

Gloria had never felt so humiliated in all her life. Even now when she was angry and hurt, she still wanted his explanation. She deserved that much.

At the knock on the door, she snapped her head up, wiped her eyes and straightened in her seat. "Come in."

For about three seconds she hoped Malcolm would be the one opening her door. However, it was Amelia's cherub face that appeared.

Her heart sank, but her smile hung firm. "Yes, Ms. Blake. What can I do for you?"

"I brought up the mail from the mailroom," she said, easing into the office.

Gloria wasn't fooled at this latest fishing attempt, either. "Thank you." She accepted the bundled stack of envelopes.

"You're welcome," Amelia said, stepping backward toward the door before she finally took the plunge. "Ms. Kingsley, um, are you all right?"

"Of course," Gloria lied. "Never better." She lowered her gaze and feigned interest in the mail. She didn't have to look at Amelia to know that the woman didn't believe her, but she'd be damned if she'd ever confess the truth.

"Well, all right," Amelia said. "I guess I'll be at my desk if you need anything."

Gloria nodded and shuffled through the envelopes.

"All right." Amelia stalled, opening the door. "I'm going."

Silence.

Amelia sighed and finally left the office.

At the soft click of the door, Gloria ended her lackluster performance and tossed the mail on the desk. Why in the hell had she bothered to come into work today? She'd only been in for two hours and it was arguably one of the longest days of her life.

She glanced at the telephone and mentally commanded Malcolm to call. The long seconds stretched into even longer minutes until she gave up.

"Screw it," she snapped. "Forget him." She wasn't going to let him ruin the rest of her day. Drawing a deep breath, Gloria reached for her water bottle and chugged half of it down. It was a sorry substitute for a stiff drink.

This was one of the reasons she'd kept men at arm's length. The games they played were so juvenile. Why in the world had she entertained the idea that Malcolm Braddock had been the one for her?

What a joke.

Gloria grabbed the first envelope on her desk and reached for her sharp letter opener. "I swear, if he was standing in front of me now…" She slid open the envelope, imagining it slicing off parts of Malcolm's anatomy.

She stewed over the list of cons for having slept with Malcolm while she unfolded the final bill for Harmon's American Express card. Tossing a careless glance over the listed charges, her eyes snagged on a peculiar charge from Carlson Travel Agency.

Her eyes scanned over to the date: July 28.

The day Harmon died.

What the hell?

Reeling, Gloria picked up the phone and called Carlson Travel Agency. While she waited for the line to pick up, she turned toward her computer and pulled up Harmon's calendar for July. She didn't see anything about a trip. *Maybe he was planning something with Evelyn?*

That was one possibility, but Harmon had always relied on her to book *any* trip—business or personal. It was a prick to her pride to think Harmon wouldn't have her handle the transaction. He'd bragged at every turn on how he relied and trusted her implicitly. Everything from calls, travel, events to calendar planning were routed through her. Harmon hadn't independently remembered a birthday, anniversary or holiday in years.

"Carlson Travel Agency. This is Michelle, how can I help you?"

"Michelle, hey. This is Gloria Kingsley over at Congressman Braddock's office. How are you?"

"Glo!" Michelle shifted out of her business voice and into her after-hours sistah-girl routine. "Girlfriend, how are you holding up over there? I've been meaning to call you since the funeral, but, honey, me and Vernon are on the skids again. You know how we do."

"Yeah. Sorry to hear that but—"

"Girl, I'm starting to think you have the right idea. Cross your legs and forget about these little boys playing at being men. You feel me?"

Had that been her motto? "Michelle, I was hoping you could help me with something."

"Sure. If I can."

Gloria picked up the American Express bill again. "I have a strange charge on Harmon's credit card bill from your agency on July 28. Do you know anything about it?"

"Ah, yeah." Gloria pictured Michelle shaking her head. "It was the same day of the accident. That was why I was so shocked when I heard the news. I was like 'Wow, I'd just talked to him that day.'"

Gloria's frown deepened. She'd almost thought there had to have been some type of mistake. "Are you sure it was Mr. Braddock?"

"Of course it was him, silly. I chatted him up to see how his fine single son, Malcolm, was doing. Now, that's a *real* man. Rich as sin, smart as all get out and fine as hell. Girl, I would toss Vernon to the curb with a quickness if I could sink my hooks in him. Too bad you two can't stand each other."

"That's not true," Gloria protested. "Not entirely."

"Oh, did something change that I don't know about?"

Open mouth, insert foot. "No. I just…um, back to this trip. Where was Harmon going?"

"Washington," Michelle answered, apparently not needing to look it up. "Booked it for that evening. Said he had some last-minute business he needed to take care of."

"Washington? Business? Why wouldn't he ask me to book it for him?"

"No clue. Oops, there's my other line. Gotta go."

"Oh, okay. Talk to you later," Gloria said, and hung up the phone, thinking. *Why would Harmon book his own flight to Washington?* She turned back to her computer and pulled up the phone number for Joe Dennis, the congressman's driver and dialed.

"Hello."

Gloria blinked at the deep, raspy voice. Did the man have a cold? "Mr. Dennis?" she questioned.

"Who's calling?"

"Gloria Kingsley. How are you?"

"Um." He coughed a few times and cleared his voice. When he spoke again, he was as clear as a bell. "What can I do for you, Ms. Kingsley?"

"Well." She hesitated, and then asked, "I was wondering if you knew anything about Mr. Braddock taking a last-minute business trip the night of his accident?"

Silence.

"Mr. Dennis?"

"Yeah, um. I think he might have mentioned something like that. I dropped him off at the mansion around 4:00 p.m. and left for the night. He said you'd call me for his pickup time."

"Huh." That didn't make a lick of sense. How could she tell Joe when to pick him up if she didn't know he was going anywhere?

"That's all I know."

Silence.

"Ms. Kingsley?"

"Yeah, okay. Thanks for your time." She disconnected the call but continued to stare at the phone. After a minute, she turned back to the computer and pulled up another number: private investigator Drey St. John. She picked up the phone, but then just as quickly hung it up. "Get a grip. You're overreacting." She laughed at herself. "It was just one ticket. It doesn't mean a thing."

Chapter 16

"Malcolm, baby! You came." Evelyn Braddock swept her arms open and embraced her oldest son.

"Well, of course I made it, Mom." He leaned forward to allow his mother to cup his face and kiss both sides of his face. "You didn't think I'd miss your birthday, did you? How have you been holding up? You look well."

A beautiful smile graced his mother's full lips. "I'm leaning on the Lord and taking it one day at a time," she said. Her eyes twinkled up at him. "The real question is how are *you* doing, baby?"

Falling apart. "I'm doing good."

His mother's eyes narrowed to study him—a sign that said she doubted his story. "Well, I'm glad you're here." She tilted her head to the side to try to see what he was hiding. "What's that behind your back?"

Malcolm straightened and presented a cube-size box, wrapped in gold-and-silver paper and graced with a red bow. "You didn't think I would forget a gift for my best girl on her special day, did you?"

Evelyn's smile remained as she shook her head. "You didn't have to buy me anything. Just having the family here is the best gift right now."

"Then, let's consider this a bonus," he said, squeezing her waist and then planting a kiss against her forehead. "Where is everybody?"

"Out in the garden. Tyson has fired up that monstrosity of a grill your father bought last year. Said he thinks he finally figured out how to make Harmon's secret barbecue sauce."

Malcolm rolled his eyes. "Now, that boy knows he doesn't know nothing about barbecuing. I better get out there before he burns down the backyard."

Evelyn chuckled. "Now, don't you two start," she warned.

For as long as Malcolm remembered, his mother's birthday marked the last summer barbecue. When Malcolm and Tyson were children, their father was named master of the grill and took credit for developing a lip-smacking special barbecue sauce that was the envy of family and friends. Sometime around when Malcolm was in college, Harmon allowed his sons to compete for the master of the grill title. The competition continued to this day, and it probably would go on for the rest of their lives.

Malcolm and his mother walked through their large family home arm in arm. It was clear that they were borrowing each other's strength to get through the day.

From the moment they stepped out on the stone-tiled patio, the smell of Tyson's barbecue caused Malcolm's stomach to growl in appreciation. However, Malcolm's competitive side made him anxious to bump his brother off the grill.

Marching around the estate's twelve-foot fountain and down the secluded walkway, Malcolm and Evelyn finally joined their family in the second courtyard in the center of the property's rich, manicured lawn. "Malcolm, you made it," Shawnie proclaimed, jumping up from her seat. Malcolm was so glad she had thawed since his last visit. She even looked better, too.

Tyson glanced up from the grill. "Here comes my competition now," he announced, wearing a ridiculous red-and-white smock that proclaimed him to be King of the Grill.

Malcolm's arm fell from his mother's waist so he could accept his sister's wide hug; however, his attention was drawn to another woman sitting serenely at the outdoor table.

"Ms. Kingsley," he greeted her with an awkward tilt of his head.

Gloria's eyebrows jumped at the formal greeting. "Malcolm. Surely by now we should be on a first-name basis," she said in a tone that was equally sweet and sour.

"Of course. You're right," he answered stiffly.

"My goodness, Malcolm," Shawnie said, easing out of his arms. "You're so tense," she noted, giving his shoulders an impromptu squeeze. "Loosen up. We're all here to have a good time on Mom's big day."

Malcolm tried to relax, but he was finding the task difficult under Gloria's glare. He didn't blame her for her open hostility. It had been nine days since that incredible night at her apartment.

Nine days since he'd felt her incredible body beneath him.

Nine days since he'd tasted her lips.

Nine days since they'd uttered a word to each other.

Nine days since he'd left her bed while she lay sleeping. He tried to brush away his guilt.

From the corner of his eyes, Malcolm saw his mother approach the table and he quickly went to pull out her chair.

"Now, don't you start doting on me," his mother chastised. "I may be getting older, but I'm not an old lady." She laughed.

"I'm just trying to be a gentleman," he told her, and kissed her cheek.

"Ah, turning over a new leaf?" Gloria chirped in sharply.

Shawnie's and Evelyn's heads snapped up and their gazes ping-ponged between Malcolm and Gloria.

Instead of participating in a war of words, Malcolm turned his attention toward Tyson—who, coincidentally, had stopped what he was doing to observe the action from the sidelines.

"So where is Felicia?" Malcolm asked, changing the subject.

"She couldn't make it." Tyson turned back toward the grill, but not before emotion rippled across his face. "She's out of town."

Concern twisted in Malcolm's gut as he approached his brother and dropped a hand on his shoulder. "Hey, man. Is everything all right?" he asked low enough for Tyson's ear only.

Tyson glanced over his shoulder, his once-troubled expression wiped clean. "Sure. Why do you ask?"

Malcolm's response was an awkward beat of silence. It was highly hypocritical of him to request his brother to open up to him when he himself had been unable to do so for the past few weeks.

He needed to do better.

"Look, Ty. If—"

"I hope you brought your appetite with you," Tyson said. "Because once you taste my new sauce, I won't be able to beat you off these ribs with a stick."

"Okay. Now you're delusional," Malcolm joked, rolling his eyes.

"So, Gloria, is it true that Clint Hardy is going to run for Dad's seat?" Shawnie asked.

Malcolm hadn't meant to, but he'd turned toward the table with a scowl.

Gloria bobbed her head. "Looks that way. He's holding a press conference Monday to make the official announcement."

Malcolm pretended he didn't feel the kick to his gut.

"Have you thought about what you're going to do after the changing of the guard?" Evelyn asked.

Gloria sighed. "I haven't made a decision yet. Clint asked whether I would be willing to stay on board—work for him."

Malcolm just stared at her.

Gloria ignored him and kept talking to his

mother. "I'm not sure if I agree on some of his ideas, but we're supposed to go out for a business dinner next week. So we'll see."

"Yeah, right. Business." Malcolm rolled his eyes.

"That's right. Business," Gloria repeated with strained patience. "And if it wasn't, I fail to see how it concerns anyone else."

"Who's concerned?"

For a moment, the small family gathering fell silent again as Malcolm and Gloria shared matching glares.

"Um, am I missing something?" Shawnie asked, setting down her glass of lemonade. "Is something going on between you two?"

Gloria laughed. "Not a thing."

That was the second kick to Malcolm's gut—even if it was of his own making.

Evelyn drew a deep breath during the ensuing silence. "So, Malcolm. What was this big announcement you hinted that you wanted to make?"

He hesitated. He hadn't planned on Gloria being there today, while in retrospect he just realized, she'd been coming to Evelyn's birthday barbecue for a few years now. "Nothing. We can talk about it later."

Gloria's delicate eyebrows climbed higher.

Shawnie, ignoring her brother's hint that he didn't want to discuss the matter in front of present company, laughed. "C'mon, Malcolm. You can talk in front of Gloria. She's practically family."

Practically family.

"Yeah, Malcolm. You know I can keep secrets." Gloria's hard gaze leveled on him.

Malcolm's chin came up as he drew a deep breath. For an insane moment, he wanted to wipe the smug and superior look off Gloria's face. Maybe it was best that she was here today. She could hear of his trip today instead of later—especially since he didn't know when "later" was going to be.

"All right," he said, his tone clipped. "I've told you all earlier this year about the Arc Foundation partnering up with World Camp's Malawi Outreach program."

All three women stiffened.

"We've finally pounded out the details, and the Arc's first group of volunteers is set to leave September 1." He paused and swung his gaze toward his mother, hoping to gauge whether she was all right with this decision. "I'll be going with them."

Gloria's jaw dropped open. "That's next week."

He nodded and watched understanding dawn in her eyes.

"So you were going to just up and leave?"

"I've been planning this trip for a long time."

"Yeah," Shawnie jumped in. "But that was before Dad passed away."

The first few cinder blocks of guilt crashed onto Malcolm's shoulders.

Shawnie continued, "I know you've been planning it for a while, but can't you go at another time? I mean—I thought you'd run for Daddy's seat."

He frowned. "You know how I feel about the whole political circus."

"Oh, please. You say that, but it isn't true. The way you and Dad would spar back and forth over ideas and policies is a testament to your passion for the very politics you claim to despise."

"Amen to that," Ty agreed, setting a heaping platter of barbecue ribs on the center of the outdoor table. "You guys would debate for hours."

"And almost always you were on the same side but differed on the right strategy."

"Forget it." Gloria cut into the family argument. "I've already tried to convince him. The only kind of running he's interested in is running away."

The zinger silenced the table once again.

Gloria hadn't meant for her temper to keep flaring, but Malcolm's *announcement* had angered her beyond her control. When she'd gone into this personal campaign to persuade Malcolm into politics, she'd known and accepted the challenges it would entail.

However, losing her heart had not been part of the deal, and it was growing harder by the second to pretend Malcolm's determined indifference wasn't tearing her in two.

Struggling not to make a scene, Gloria quickly excused herself from the table and willed herself not to run the long way back to the main house. Instead, she strolled calmly with her head held high and her shoulders straight. She had no doubt that Malcolm's heavy gaze followed her, but she was determined not to lose what little pride she had left.

By the time she made it to the bathroom on the main floor, she'd given up the fight and allowed her tears to flow down her face.

He was leaving. He was actually going to leave. Had that night truly meant nothing to him?

Gloria closed her eyes in anguish, and her treacherous mind replayed images from that glorious night—just as it had done for the past nine days.

"Why did I even bother coming here?" she moaned under her breath. The only answer was that she was a glutton for punishment. Somehow she'd convinced herself that once Malcolm saw her again, she could force him to face his feelings for her—or at least *talk* to her.

Something.

Something that confirmed that she'd not imagined the passion in which he'd made love to her or the desire she'd tasted from his lips. Surely she hadn't imagined all of that.

Instead, all she'd seen was Malcolm's fierce determination to get away from her.

The tears gushed and it was a long while before she finally managed to pull it together. Finally, she marched over to the stone-and-marble vanity area and winced at the mess she'd made of herself. There was no way she was going to let him see her like this.

Quickly, she fixed her hair and makeup. When she finished, she convinced herself, or rather prayed, no one would notice the red tint of her eyes or the puffiness of her nose. One thing for sure, she was determined to get through this evening with her dignity intact. When she returned to the barbecue, Malcolm had somehow managed to bump Tyson off the grill and was busy teaching him the best way to lock flavor into the meat.

She knew exactly when his gaze had shifted toward her, but she was determined to prove that she knew how to ignore him, too. Plus, she knew just the right button to push to get under his skin.

Clint Hardy.

It was childish and juvenile, but Gloria couldn't

help herself. After talking about him for a while, she rather enjoyed watching Malcolm grind his teeth, or how his muscles ticked along his jawline.

Soon, Shawnie picked up on her little game and decided to help her. Gloria recalled every asinine point or detail Hardy had brought up at Cayman's fund-raiser. And Shawnie chimed in thinking friendly competition would spur him on.

Malcolm started burning the meat. Tyson jumped in, laughing, and reclaimed his throne.

"Well, he stands a good chance in winning a lot of female votes," Shawnie said. "The man should be in Hollywood, not politics."

"I didn't know you had a thing for Clint Hardy," Evelyn commented, surprised.

"I don't," Shawnie said. "I'm just saying that the man is easy on the eyes."

"That's putting it mildly," Gloria volleyed back with her friend.

"Please tell me that's not all it takes for a man to win your vote," Tyson cut in.

"No. Not all," Shawnie shot back. "But it certainly doesn't hurt. Doesn't it, Gloria?"

"Not at all."

Malcolm grunted.

The rest of the birthday barbecue became an odd mixture of laughter, reminiscent silence and occasional hostile quips between Malcolm and Gloria. Evelyn opened her small pile of presents and grew weepy when Gloria presented her with a silver locket Harmon had bought her prior to his death.

As evening descended, the small family gathering moved back into the mansion where reams of photos were pulled out and memories were shared.

The hour grew late and Evelyn started releasing a series of yawns that grew wider and longer. "As much as I hate to end this night," Evelyn said, "it's time for me to go to bed."

Everyone glanced at their watches, noting how late it was.

Evelyn stood and kissed each of them good-night.

"Malcolm, sweetheart, you make sure you come back by before you leave on your trip."

"I will, Mama." He kissed her again.

Evelyn moved toward Gloria, who was sliding her purse strap over her shoulder. "Thank you so much for coming. I hope this won't be your last visit here."

"It won't be," Gloria said, but had a sinking feeling that it would.

Evelyn took her into her arms and whispered in her ear. "Don't give up on him, baby."

The encouragement shocked Gloria, but before she could utter a response, Evelyn swept from the room.

Shawnie hooked an arm around her brother Tyson and ordered him to walk her to her car, instantly leaving Gloria and Malcolm alone in the room.

After the humiliation she'd suffered all day, the last thing Gloria wanted was to be alone with him. She quickly turned and marched out of the room, hoping to catch up with Shawnie and Tyson.

"That's it? You're not even going to say goodbye?" Malcolm said, walking behind her.

"Just following your example," she tossed over her shoulder without slowing her pace. "I'm surprised you didn't leave skid marks on the carpet when you left my apartment."

"I'm sorry about that."

Gloria rounded on him, fire in her eyes. "Are you?" she challenged. "It was sort of hard to tell since you didn't even have the decency to call me."

Malcolm's jaw worked while his own anger simmered.

"Keep your apologies," she hissed, and turned on her heel. "I don't want them or you." Gloria had only taken two steps into the darkened foyer when Malcolm's hand clamped around her arm and dragged her into the shadows.

"Take your hands off me," she snapped.

"Will you shut up and listen?" he growled.

"I don't want to listen. I don't want to hear

anything you have to say. That night was a mistake. The biggest one I've ever made."

In a flash his body pressed against hers. "Don't say that. You don't mean it."

Her tears flowed. "How could you just ignore me like that? Didn't that night mean anything to you?"

"Of course it did." His voice cracked as if he was experiencing internal breakdown.

"Then why?"

Because I'm not sure if you want me or the man you want me to be. "It's complicated," he admitted, regretting the hurt he'd caused her.

"Then let me uncomplicate things for you," she said, mopping her tears with the back of her hands. "Let me go."

He wanted to, but he just couldn't. Instead he kissed her.

And then he wanted more.

Chapter 17

Gloria hated Malcolm...but, oh, how she loved him, too.

If she'd ever questioned that, her body's response to him now had finally given her its answer. Seconds ago, she was determined to march out of his life forever. Now she couldn't imagine a world without him. What else could explain them pulling at each other's clothes in the shadows of the main entryway where just a sliver of light streamed through the glass and wrought-iron?

"Oh, God. Do you know what you do to me?"

Malcolm panted in a ragged whisper that hinted that he was just seconds from exploding.

Hell, did he know what he did to her? Her heart hammered hard against her rib cage and her blood boiled to the point where her entire body felt feverish. None of that mattered as long as Malcolm's kisses intoxicated her and his hands stroked and caressed her puckered nipples.

Gloria surrendered to her riotous feelings and willingly handed her heart to a man who'd in all likelihood shatter it into a million pieces. Yet, she didn't care. All that mattered was this small window in time when he wanted her as much as she wanted him.

Oh, how much she wanted him.

She slid her legs against his, caressed them for a few strokes to hint what she craved. She didn't feel when the button of her white shorts opened nor when her zipper slid down. However, she was acutely aware when her shorts and panties were peeled off her hips.

Hearing the condom packet rip open, Gloria just barely had time to grab Malcolm's broad shoulders and hold on before he lifted her off the ground and plunged inside her.

Air rushed from her lungs, his thick shaft filling her completely. At his first strokes, tears rose and leaked from the corners of her eyes. Nothing had ever felt so exquisite.

Somewhere in the distance, a door opened.

Malcolm and Gloria froze.

The panic in Gloria's heart didn't come from the possibility of getting caught in a compromising position, but from the fear that Malcolm would come to his senses and not finish what he'd started.

Light footsteps shuffled across the marble floor while a feminine hum filled the bottom floor.

It was Sarona—likely grabbing a night snack before heading off to bed.

Gloria and Malcolm held their breaths. What if she came to check the front door? The seconds stretched for what seemed like an eternity. The air pinned in Gloria's chest burned.

At long last, the foyer lights were turned off; except for a few streams of moonlight, the bottom floor was pitched into darkness.

Gloria finally exhaled in relief; but then Sarona walked past the entryway, sandwich in hand, and fear seized her. Malcolm's and Gloria's gazes followed Sarona as she hummed and wiggled her hips. Through the moonlight, Gloria was able to make out the white iPod earplugs jammed into her ears.

Even before the petite older woman climbed up the stairs, Malcolm began to move inside her—a slow grind that caused Gloria's eyes to roll toward the ceiling. In no time her breathing turned rapid and shallow. The petals of her pending orgasm opened slowly.

Malcolm bent forward, drawing a sensitive breast into his hot mouth. She moaned.

Malcolm now knew what insanity was like. Why when she was just seconds from walking out of his life did he drag her back in? He didn't remember thinking.

When Sarona had made her untimely appearance while they were hiding in the dark like two hormonally charged teenagers, he could have ended this madness. But he lacked the strength to withdraw—especially while her inner muscles squeezed him so. To pull out would have been like amputating a limb or carving out his heart.

None of this made sense.

He hated her…but, oh, how he loved her, too.

Love. There was that word again, echoing and bouncing around inside his head. He shook his head—not wanting to analyze anything. He just wanted to enjoy this moment.

This would be their last time, he promised. He just wanted this last time. Lord knows that she didn't love him. She loved the idea of what she wanted him to be. Right?

One last time and then it would be over.

He moaned deep in his throat as their bodies' friction ignited a blazing fire.

Gloria gasped, her eyes wide as her body quaked violently with her climax.

Malcolm drove deep into her wet heat until ecstasy consumed him.

As time passed, sweat cooled their bodies, and still he held her pinned to the wall panting in the crook of her neck and inhaling the scent of her skin. Reality parted the euphoric clouds in his head when she whispered, "I love you."

He closed his eyes; his heart hardened.

"Don't leave," she begged softly. "Stay here and be with me." Her hands lifted and cupped his face. "Your place is here."

He lifted his head, met her stare in the moonlight. "Why? So I can take my father's place?"

Her question filled her gaze before she uttered, "Would that be so bad?"

"You just don't get it, do you?" His lips quirked with a half smile. "You don't love me," he said. "You just love your idea of me. The idea of me being my father."

Gloria frowned. "That's not true."

He backed away and fixed his clothes. "This could never work. *We* could never work." It hurt like hell to watch the tears surface in her eyes, but this was something he had to do. "Goodbye, Gloria."

Chapter 18

Monday morning, Gloria returned to work looking as if she'd spent the whole weekend crying—which she had. What was left of Harmon's skeletal crew had all steered clear of her and her noticeable mood swings. At lunchtime, everyone gathered into the break room to watch Clint Hardy announce his run for congressional office.

Gloria's heart twisted in disappointment, but it was time to concede her defeat—in more ways than one. Before she knew it, her mind tangled with thoughts of Malcolm despite her constant vows not to think of him. Her mind replayed every moment they'd spent together since Harmon's death.

In a way, she could understand why Malcolm believed her feelings extended to just his political potential. What else could he have thought when every time she opened her mouth she was urging him to continue his father's legacy? Did she once stop to appreciate who Malcolm Braddock was—his hard dedication to his own beliefs in what was right and wrong?

She should have told him every chance she could about how much she admired his work and kind heart. Malcolm was an intelligent and caring man— who'd give anyone the shirt off his back if they were in need. Why did she have to badger him right on the heels of his incredible loss?

No. She'd made him feel like he wasn't good enough, his work wasn't good enough, when he already did more than most.

The press conference ended and a news anchor went on to report something about Stewart Industries when Mabel touched her on the shoulder.

"Ms. Kingsley, are you all right?"

Gloria blinked out of her reverie and noticed that the break room had emptied out. She hung an awkward smile on her face as she cleared her throat. "Yes, yes. I just had a lot of things on my mind. I better get back to work."

While most things were at a standstill until the district elected their new congressman, it didn't stop the overwhelming amount of paperwork from flowing in. Lawmakers and their constituents faxed and shipped in proposals while taxpayers mailed and e-mailed complaints or praises about one thing or another—and Gloria still received a few letters and cards of condolences for their previous representative.

Now, within minutes of Hardy's announcement, Gloria's phone started ringing off the hook. Everyone, it seemed, wanted to be the first on the new representative's schedule—whoever it might be.

Gloria welcomed anything that would keep her busy—anything that would prevent her from obsessing over how much she missed what she never had with Malcolm. Sometime around two o'clock, her head started to ache and her stomach growled. A small reminder that she'd worked through lunch.

At the rap on her door, Gloria barked, "Come in," without looking up.

Mabel poked her head into the office. "Mail," she said, breezing inside and then dropping a thick stack of envelopes on the desk.

"Thanks," Gloria said, still refusing to make eye contact.

"I also brought you this." Mabel set an orange and a granola bar down on the desk. "Even Superman had to eat."

The first genuine smile of the day touched Gloria's lips. "Thanks, Mabel. You're a lifesaver."

Mabel left the office with a smile and Gloria quickly attacked her light snack. After a few healthy bites, she slumped back into her seat, sated but not satisfied.

Her eyes drifted to the mail. Since the unusual ticket purchase, Gloria found herself combing every bill meticulously. What was she looking for? She had no idea. But it was *something*.

So far, her paranoia had turned out to be just that. Maybe that was a good thing—especially since she had come so close to calling a private investigator. Grabbing her trusty letter opener, Gloria ripped into Harmon's final cell phone bill. She immediately frowned because it was considerably higher than normal. She shook her head after one glance at the excessive charges.

Remembering the call to Carlson Travel Agency, Gloria flipped the bill over and scanned for July 28. And there it was. That settled it. He *had* made that call.

A part of her still couldn't believe he hadn't delegated the task to her. She almost set the bill aside for the next envelope when she noticed the other numbers from that day.

One number in particular, mainly because it seemed to be everywhere, stood out. She flipped through the pages and the number was listed almost on every page. What was even stranger was that Gloria didn't recognize the number—and she knew just about everyone Harmon dealt with on a day-to-day basis.

She frowned and almost absently turned in her seat toward her computer. A few keystrokes and she pulled up her electronic address book and keyed in the number for a search.

Nothing came up.

Gloria's paranoia returned, but she tried her best to dismiss it. After all, a busy man like Harmon Braddock made new contacts nearly every day. It could be nothing more than a business contact. Leaning back in her chair, she tried to accept that perfectly logical explanation.

When that didn't work, she flipped through the bill a second time. Finally her curiosity won out and she picked up the phone, dialed the number and held her breath.

"Thank you for calling Stewart Industries. How may I direct your call?"

Gloria frowned. "I'm sorry. I must have dialed

the wrong number," she said, and then hung up. However, she continued to stare at the phone. Why on earth was Harmon calling Stewart Industries?

Harmon Braddock wasn't a big oil fan, despite Evelyn's family making their fortune in oil. Was the company trying to woo the congressman?

Stewart Industries hosted Senator Cayman's political fund-raiser a couple of weeks ago. Maybe it had something to do with that? If so, why didn't she know about it? And why was he calling a switchboard and not a direct number within the company?

Gloria stared at the phone, thinking.

Malcolm also chose to bury himself in work. He spent his morning presenting a check to the Texas Children's Cancer Center. With the final totals in from their July fund-raising concert, it felt good to hand over a two-million-dollar check.

A few cameras and photographers from the local media covered the presentation. Orville Roark took the podium and read the center's mission statement and urged the public to join forces and get involved. Malcolm was next to step up to the microphone, and he gently reminded everyone what the Arc Foundation was all about.

"Mr. Braddock," a faceless reporter called out.

"What do you think of Clint Hardy's announcement to run for your father's seat in Congress?"

Malcolm froze. The question caught him off guard. After a few pictures snapped, he put on his best smile and responded, "I wish Mr. Hardy well in all his political endeavors."

"Mr. Braddock, have you given any thought to running for your father's seat?" the reporter pried.

Malcolm elected to answer honestly. "The subject has come up." Unfortunately, he regretted his candor when a new energy buzzed among the reporters.

"Does that mean that you're going to be making your own announcement soon?"

"I'm sorry, but that's all for now. Thank you all for coming." Malcolm forced on another smile and rushed from the podium.

Reporters fired off questions at his back as he exited the conference room.

"I'm sorry about that," Malcolm said to Roark. "I didn't mean to turn the focus from the center."

"Don't be." Roark waved off the apology. "I'm actually pleased to hear you're considering running. We need a man like you in Congress. I think your father would be proud."

Malcolm chuckled. "So everyone keeps telling me."

"And you doubt it?"

* * *

An hour later, Malcolm stared at his father's name etched in gray marble. His eyes stung with invisible tears while his heart constricted painfully in his chest. When would the blocks of regret be lifted from his shoulders? What if it never went away?

Even now he had so much to say and didn't know where to start. Then, at long last, he just began talking. "I always thought that there was plenty of time," he said. "Plenty of time for us to cool down. Plenty of time for me to find my way. Plenty of time to fall in love." Malcolm lowered his head. "Turns out that was the biggest lie I've ever told myself.

"I love you, Dad." He sighed. "I'm at a crossroads. I keep finding myself floundering," he admitted. "I always thought I wanted one thing, but now I'm thinking I want something else. It's strange to have so many people see something within you that you don't even see yourself."

As tears burned the backs of his eyes, Malcolm tilted his head toward the sky while he tried to compose himself. When he was ready, his gaze returned to his father's grave.

"I've always believed in the work I was doing, always had a sense of pride while doing it. But now…seeds have been planted inside my head that I could do more—be more. And I'll be damned if I can shake them out. They've taken root and it makes me wonder if everybody is right." He paused. "You always believed that I would follow in your footsteps, didn't you?" A sad laugh tumbled from his lips. "My hero. My Eliot Ness."

A montage of happy childhood memories flashed inside his head. The hole inside his heart enlarged. "I'm sorry, Dad. That fight we had… God, it seems so stupid to me now. Maybe Mom had the right of it. We were both just so stubborn." Malcolm shook his head while his confession tumbled out. "Now someone else believes in me. Turns out you and Mom may have been right about her, too. I don't know. I'm nowhere near figuring any of this out. But I'm suddenly afraid of running out of time."

Silence hung on the air while Malcolm squatted beside the tombstone, kissed his fingers and placed them against his father's name. "I miss you, Dad. Whatever I decide to do, I hope you'll continue to be proud." He stood and walked back to his SUV. As he approached, he was surprised to see Tyson leaning against the hood.

"Figured I'd find you here."

"What—are you a psychic?"

"No. I just know you. You're not as deep as you think you are." Tyson crooked up a side of his lips.

"Ha. Ha."

"Came to tell the old man you were shipping out?"

"You can say that." Malcolm pulled out his car keys and then folded his arms. "Is there a reason you tracked me down?"

"Wanted to talk."

"About?"

"Your trip to Malawi. Wanted to find out for myself what you're running from."

Malcolm laughed, though it didn't quite sound right to his own ears. "I'm not running from anything."

"No? I'd say you were running from someone about five-eight, short light brown hair with golden highlights and gold eyes."

Malcolm rolled his eyes. "You don't know what you're talking about."

"I am many things, bro. But blind is not one of them—and one would have to be to miss the sparks flying off you and Gloria. C'mon. What gives?"

"What? You're going to counsel me on relationships?"

Tyson's jaw hardened.

Malcolm regretted the jab. "Sorry. Look, it's just complicated."

"And Malawi is going to uncomplicate things?"

"A man can hope."

"You know, this past month, I barely recognize

you, man. You've always been so independent and strong. Now…"

"I'm floundering." Malcolm repeated the words he'd said at his father's grave. "Dad's death…"

"It's really shaken you up."

"I've lost my way," he admitted.

"And how does Gloria feel about you?" Tyson asked.

Malcolm hesitated. "She says she loves me."

Tyson's brows climbed upward. "You don't believe her?"

Drawing a deep breath, Malcolm weighed his words carefully. "I don't know what I believe. When I'm with her, I feel there's nothing I can't do, but then I wonder…"

"About?"

"Does she love me or the idea of resurrecting Dad?"

"Come again?"

Malcolm sighed. "Let's just say Gloria was Dad's number-one fan. She idolized the man, and I can't help but think her only interest in me is turning me into her idol."

Ty released a long steady breath. "Okay. Now, that's deep." He waited a beat. "But it doesn't sound like the Gloria I know. Maybe you should talk to her about it."

Malcolm thought about the way he'd ended things with Gloria. "I think we're way past talking."

Gloria emerged from her thoughts and picked up the phone. After punching in Joe Dennis's phone number, she drummed her fingers on the desk and tried to arrange the questions inside her head.

"Hello."

"Joe?" She perked up. "Hi. It's Gloria Kingsley again…from Harmon Braddock's office?"

Silence.

"Um, I was just wondering if you had a few minutes to talk?"

"Depends on what you want to talk about."

"Well, actually, I was wondering if you ever took Mr. Braddock to Stewart Industries."

Silence.

"Hello?"

"Ms. Kingsley, Mr. Braddock is dead. Why don't you leave well enough alone."

Click.

Gloria pulled the phone from her ear and frowned at it. "Leave well enough alone? What in the hell does that mean?"

Chapter 19

Malcolm returned to his apartment and invited his brother inside. After their talk at the grave site, the two decided they needed a beer. It felt good to hang out and detangle some of his troubled thoughts—though he couldn't say the same for his brother.

"So are you all packed?" Tyson asked.

"For the most part," Malcolm said. "I still need to get a couple things. Probably get to it tomorrow."

Tyson bobbed his head.

Malcolm walked into the kitchen and retrieved two beers from the refrigerator.

"Thanks, man. Nothing like a cold one at the end of the day, huh?"

Malcolm nodded and clicked the bottles together in a silent toast.

Tyson took a long pull as if he hadn't had a beer in eons, and then tossed a smile over at Malcolm. "I really wish you would reconsider your trip. Five weeks is a long time."

"It's not that long."

"Long enough to change things."

"Hopefully for the better."

"Do you really think that?"

Malcolm frowned, but instead of answering, he took a long pull from his beer, as well.

"Can I ask you something?"

"Shoot."

"Brother to brother. Man to man. Why won't you consider running for Dad's seat?"

He groaned. "Ah, man. Not you, too."

"It's a legitimate question. Why?"

"Why not you?"

"Come on, man. For you and Dad, politics is in your blood—whether you want to admit it or not. Shawnie was right. The way you guys argued and debated the issues. You have a real passion for it. But it seems like you go out of your way to deny it because…what? Clue me in."

Malcolm didn't have an answer to give him. He never had an answer for his dad, either. He set his beer down on the kitchen counter—perhaps a little harder than he intended. "Why is it that everyone thinks they know what I want better than I do?"

"That's actually a very good question. How come you don't know what you want?"

Malcolm blinked for having the question launched back at him.

"Well? What do you want?"

"I want…to be a person that brings about real change in the world. To do that, I believe that you have to get your hands dirty. Sure I could go to Congress and toss out rhetoric and watch change happen at a snail's pace, and most times not for the better."

Tyson shrugged. "Why can't you do both? Just because you're a congressman, it doesn't mean that your charitable work has to stop. Nobody is saying you have to stop being you, Malcolm. It's just time for you to go to the next level. Yours and Dad's ideals were very similar…and, yes, I know he disappointed you in some of his decisions, but he did some great work, too. You can't deny that. You just had different ideas about how to go about effecting change. Dad thought you'd follow in his footsteps. I think you should, too. Just take that passion to the next level."

The phone rang.

Malcolm groaned but made no attempt to answer it.

"Screening your phone calls?"

"I'll call whoever it is later," he said, his eyes locked on the cordless across the room.

The call transferred to his answering machine.

"Malcolm? Are you there? Please pick up. It's Gloria."

Malcolm lowered his head and took another swig of beer.

Tyson leveled a gaze on his brother.

Gloria's voice continued to filter over the speakerphone. "All right, then. When you get this message, please call me back. I need to talk with you. It's important." She hung up.

Tyson shook his head.

"No lectures," Malcolm warned, sensing that one was on the horizon.

"I'm not going to say anything."

Tyson's cell phone rang. He scooped the phone from his pocket and flipped it open. "Hello." His eyes scanned back to his brother. "Well, hi, Gloria." A beat. "Malcolm? Why, sure I have. I'm at his place. He's sitting right here next to me." With a wicked smile, he held out his phone. "It's for you."

Malcolm glared at his younger brother.

"What? You didn't say I couldn't answer my phone."

Malcolm snatched the phone. "Hello."

"Malcolm, thank goodness. I have to talk to you."

Malcolm turned, giving his brother his back. "Gloria, I really don't think that's a good idea. I think we said all we had to say to each other the other night."

There was a small pause before Gloria's voice came back onto the line. "It's not about that. It's—"

"Gloria, this is hard enough. Please. Let's just step away from this. Okay? I have to go. Goodbye." He flipped the phone closed before he lost his courage and changed his mind.

"I don't think you have a clue as to what you're doing—what you're about to throw away."

"No lectures, remember?"

Tyson tossed up his hands. "Whatever, man." He stood, set his empty beer bottle down on the counter. "I'm heading out. I'll catch up with you later." He headed toward the door.

Malcolm remained on his stool at the breakfast bar.

Tyson opened the front door, stopped and turned. "You remember that thing you were saying about regret?"

Malcolm looked up.

"You better hope that this Gloria situation

doesn't turn into something else you'll spend the rest of your life regretting. I don't think you'll be able to handle that." With one final look of warning, Tyson turned and walked out of the apartment.

Malcolm sighed and drained the rest of his beer.

The moment Malcolm hung up one her, Gloria jumped up from behind her desk, crammed the cell phone and credit card bills into her satchel and raced out of her office. Who in the hell did Malcolm Braddock think he was?

She had dealt with men with serious egos before, but Malcolm had finally crossed the line.

Hanging up on her. Had he lost his mind?

Gloria jumped into her Mini Cooper and sped out of the parking lot. Car horns blared from all directions as she crisscrossed through traffic, ran through yellow lights and flipped a series of birds to drivers who refused to let her merge.

By the time she made it to Malcolm's apartment building, she was a ball of fury.

Hang up on her. She'd teach him.

Malcolm needed to finish packing, but he had no more than pulled his luggage out onto the bed when he decided he needed a second beer. Drinking, he found himself back in the living room replaying that old campaign footage. He listened to his father's speeches, feeling inspiration in his words. Like he'd done many times this past month, when Gloria's face came onto the screen, he froze the frame and studied her beautiful profile.

You better hope that this Gloria situation doesn't turn into something else you'll spend the rest of your life regretting.

Malcolm was already regretting a lot of things. He regretted ever having held her, kissed her, and he certainly regretted making love to her, because now those images tormented him and his body craved her touch damn near every minute of the day. He was in hell.

He turned his gaze to the phone. Maybe he should call. He shouldn't have hung up on her like that. However, a part of him didn't want to draw out the inevitable breakup. Unless she loved him for who he was and not some ideological version of his father, they had no future. That thought broke his heart—mainly because he was already in love with her. Had been since the first time he'd laid eyes on her. He had created his indifference to her in his mind for so many years because he wouldn't allow himself to believe in love at first sight, and he had hated that she'd seemed more smitten with his father than him.

Before his rift with his father, Malcolm rather enjoyed their volleying quips whenever he visited his father's office. And Lord knew it was impossible not to notice how a room's temperature would jump whenever they were together.

He studied Gloria's smile on the TV screen, and then closed his eyes to recall the sound of her laughter the few times she'd let down her guard to actually relax. But none of that compared to how he felt whenever she was in his arms. Somehow, she always felt like home.

Bam! Bam! Bam!

Malcolm's front door jumped and rattled.

"Who on earth?" Malcolm stood from the sofa and went to answer the door. Seconds before he could reach it, the door jumped again. "Who is it?"

"Open this damn door," Gloria barked.

Malcolm frowned. This certainly didn't sound good.

He opened the door and Gloria stormed inside, jabbing a finger into the center of his chest.

"How dare you hang up on me!" she shouted. "I've had enough of you being an arrogant ass."

Malcolm could do no more than blink at the ball of fire in front of him. He'd never seen her so angry. She'd never looked so passionate or so beautiful.

"If you don't want to run for Congress—fine! If

you don't want me—fine! But one thing you won't do is disrespect me. You got that?"

Shooting his hands up in surrender, Malcolm knew when he was defeated. "You're right. I was wrong. I shouldn't have hung up on you."

The apology seemed to cool her temper a little— very little. Gloria straightened her shoulders. "That's better." She drew a breath. "Now. I didn't call about us or whatever we were. I called because…there's been a few irregularities going on at the office."

Malcolm's expression twisted in confusion. "What do you mean, irregularities?"

Gloria snatched open her satchel and shoved the papers at him.

"What's this?

"Credit card bills and cell phone bills."

"What? You want me to pay them or something?"

"Don't be ridiculous," she snapped. "A couple of weeks ago I received Harmon's final American Express bill and there was a charge from Carlson Travel Agency."

"Yeah. And?"

"I didn't make the charge. I called the agency and apparently your father booked a flight to Washington the day he died."

"Why was he going to Washington?"

"That's what I'd like to know. I handled all your father's travel arrangements. In fact, I handled everything pertaining to his personal and business scheduling. Plus, we have a separate account for travel. Why would he use his American Express card? And why not tell me about it? What if I had a conflicting event on his schedule?"

Malcolm shrugged. He didn't know much about his father's business habits. "I'm sure there was a logical explanation."

"Then there is the cell phone bill."

"What about it?"

"There's one number Harmon called a lot—Stewart Industries. He even called there the day he died. I called the number and it's a basic switchboard line. You'd think he'd have a direct number to an office or something. Then…"

"There's more."

"Well, I'd completely forgotten about it, but I received a call about a week after the funeral. It was weird. The caller just said, 'It wasn't an accident.'"

"What wasn't an accident?"

"I don't know. I just thought it was a prank. Now I'm not so sure."

"What—you think the caller was talking about my father's car accident?"

"Honestly?" she said. "I don't know what I think

anymore. First I thought I was just being paranoid, but now I just have this feeling that something's not right."

Malcolm paced a bit. "I don't know, Gloria. The police report didn't find any foul play. It was a single-car accident. As far as the call, I don't know. Maybe someone was just playing a joke on you. There are a lot of heartless bastards out there who would get off on this sort of thing."

"Then there's Joe Dennis," she said.

Malcolm's chest deflated. "What about him?"

"He was acting all weird. The first time I called him—after I received the credit card bill—I asked him if he knew anything about the trip, he said that he dropped your father off at the mansion around 4:00 p.m. and that Harmon told him I'd call with his pickup time. How was I going to call him about a pickup time when I didn't even know he was going anywhere?"

Malcolm ran his hand over his head. "Maybe he was confused."

"I called him again today when I received the cell phone bill. I asked whether he'd ever taken Harmon out to Stewart Industries, and you know what he said? He told me to *leave well enough alone*. What the hell does that mean?"

"I don't know." Malcolm shook his head and sighed. "Maybe you're blowing things out of proportion."

"What—you think I'm a complete nut job now? I don't know whether or not I'm in love with you, and now I don't know when my former boss was behaving oddly?" She snatched back the papers. "Just forget it. I don't know why I bothered you in the first place. You're too busy trying to run away from me."

"I'm not running—"

"Spare me," she hissed, and rolled her eyes. "Like I've said before, when things get hot you run out the door. You ran away from your father, your destiny and now me. I thought about that line of b.s. you hurled at me about loving the idea of you. It's not true. Thing is, I think I loved you from the beginning. Just like I think you've always loved me. That, or you just like having my picture up on your television screen every time I come over."

Malcolm turned his head and saw her image still frozen on the screen.

"Sure, I wanted you to take your father's place as congressman," she said, bringing his attention back to her. "Sue me. But as far as my feelings for you, I didn't care if you were a congressman or a garbage man. I love you because I thought you were a man of integrity. I love your big heart and how much you invest yourself into your charities and foundation. Hell, I even feel guilty for being mad about you running off to Malawi when I know it's just to help people. But forgive me if I want you here for me."

"Gloria—"

"No." Gloria opened the door. "You've walked out on me too many times this month. This time, it's my turn." Pivoting on her heels, Gloria stormed out and slammed the door behind her.

Chapter 20

Stunned, Malcolm stared at the door.

You better hope that this Gloria situation doesn't turn into something else you'll spend the rest of your life regretting.

"Gloria!" Malcolm bolted out of his reverie and snatched open the front door. The hall was empty. He turned in time to see her step inside the elevator. "Gloria!" He took off after her and caught just a flash of her tilting up her chin and her stony expression as the steel doors slid shut.

"Damn." He slapped a hand against the door and then bolted toward the stairwell. He flew down the stairs, hanging on to the rail to keep his balance. Despite taking the stairs two at a time, Malcolm feared he wasn't going fast enough. His heart beat somewhere in the pit of his stomach, tangled among knots of fear.

What have I done? The thought floated across his head. Why had it taken for her to slam the door in his face for him to clear his mind?

I didn't care if you were a congressman or a garbage man. I loved you.

Loved. Past tense.

He'd just made the biggest mistake in his life, and the best thing that had ever happened to him was likely gone forever.

Malcolm finally reached the bottom floor and jetted out of the stairwell like a speeding bullet. *Where is she?* His head spun around, hoping he'd made it to the bottom floor before she had. As he passed by the elevator, he noticed the compartment empty.

As he raced out of the building, his next play was to reach her before she made it to her car. But as he rushed into the parking lot, he spotted her Mini Cooper pull out of a parking space.

"Gloria!" Malcolm's legs picked up speed.

Unfortunately, Gloria put the pedal to the metal. A small white cloud jetted out of the tailpipe as her tires squealed and she sped out of the parking lot.

Car horns blared in her wake. No way was he going
to be able to catch up with her.

"Damn."

Tears streamed down Gloria's face while her
heartbeat pounded in her ears. "Screw him and his
'I don't need anybody' attitude," she spat at her re-
flection in the rearview mirror. She backhanded a
few tears, but they were quickly replaced by a fresh
stream, pouring from the fractured wells of her soul.

Why in the hell had she admitted that she loved
him again? Why continue to give him the power to
keep breaking her heart?

Malcolm had always been a loner. She knew that.
He'd always marched to the beat of his own drum.
She knew that, too. So why was any of this a
surprise? She knew all along that when it came to
their relationship, they were like oil and water.

They just didn't mix.

"Just pull yourself together," she coached herself.
"No man is worth your tears," she reminded herself,
thinking of the days her mother would cry over her
deadbeat dad. Hadn't she promised herself that she
would never allow a man to hurt her?

And yet…losing Malcolm seemed worthy of her
tears.

For so long, she'd kept her life nice and orderly.

She devoted her time and heart to her career. Work filled up her time to the point she never noticed how lonely she was. Her heart was locked safe behind a glass wall; but in these past few weeks, that glass had shattered and its sharp pieces had pierced her heart.

Her heartbreak felt like a long agonizing death. If this was love, she wanted nothing to do with it. It hurt too much.

Gloria made a forty-minute ride across town in twenty minutes. When she jumped out of her car and stormed toward her apartment building, she tried her best to hang on to her anger. It was all she had to buffet her pain, but it was slowly ebbing away. The pain grew more intense.

Gloria caught a few curious stares as she breezed onto the elevator and then down the hallway to her apartment. She didn't care. Let them see that she wasn't always pulled together. She wasn't always calm, cool and efficient.

In her apartment, she tumbled onto the bed—a sobbing heap, an emotional wreck. As she gathered the pile of pillows, Gloria's body trembled with earth-quaking sobs.

The phone rang.

Gloria lifted her head to stare at the phone by the bed. Malcolm's name appeared on the caller ID.

The call transferred to voice mail and Malcolm's

voice boomed into the bedroom. "Gloria, are you there? If you're there, pick up. Call me back. We need to talk."

Now he wants to talk?

Gloria plopped her head back onto the pillows and closed her eyes. "I hate him. I hate him," she cried. Maybe if she said it enough times, it would be true.

Malcolm slammed the phone down and paced his living room. All the emotions he'd tried to suppress now bubbled to the surface as he paced around the room. Gloria's face remained frozen on the television screen. There had to be a way for him to fix this.

Why was it when it came to helping people through his charity work, he was a master in his field? But when it came to his personal life, he was clueless. How was it possible to grow up in such a loving household, where he witnessed the love between his parents, and then be so inept at following their example?

Malcolm picked up the phone again and dialed Paula's number. They would have to find someone else to take his place on the Malawi trip. There was no way he was leaving now. No way could he leave things the way they were between him and Gloria. He had to win her back.

Starting toward his bedroom to find his Black-Berry, Malcolm stepped on a sheet of paper. He bent down and picked it up. It was one of the pages of the credit card bill. He glanced at the airline charge and frowned.

Was it so odd for his father to make his own travel arrangements? He had to admit he'd never known his father to do that. Malcolm thought about his own relationship with Paula and couldn't remember the last time he'd handled his own travel arrangements, either. Surely his father, a much busier man, would clear a business trip with his assistant.

Grabbing his BlackBerry out of his jacket, Malcolm scrolled through his address book and found Joe Dennis's phone number. Maybe he needed to hear Joe's explanation for himself. He punched the call button and waited. On the fourth ring the call was transferred to voice mail. Malcolm hung up.

"Okay, he's not answering his phone," he mumbled under his breath. "No big deal. I rarely answer mine." Malcolm moved to the breakfast bar, sat down and stared at the credit card bill. Why was his father going to Washington? He shrugged. He could be meeting with anyone, but why wouldn't he tell Gloria? It kept coming back to that.

Malcolm dialed Gloria's number again, and

again he was transferred to voice mail. Scrolling through his address book, he found her cell phone number and called it.

No answer.

Malcolm jumped off the stool, paced. Finally he decided to drive to Gloria's apartment. Anything was better than waiting.

As he made his way to his vehicle, his mind turned with the words he needed to apologize. He didn't deserve her now. His actions in the past two weeks were unforgivable. Apologizing wouldn't be enough, he decided. He would likely have to beg for forgiveness. And he was totally prepared to do that.

When his cell phone rang, hope bloomed in his heart as he scrambled to answer it. "Gloria?"

Silence crackled over the line, and then, "No, it's me, Shawnie."

In the blink of an eye, Malcolm's hope dissipated. "Is there a problem?"

"No, no," he lied. As he was getting ready to rush her off the phone, he decided to run some of Gloria's concerns by his sister. "Shawnie, have you ever known Dad to book his own travel arrangements?"

Shawnie laughed. "Dad? Not likely. He relied on Gloria to take care of things like that. She ran that office like a well-oiled machine."

The wheels in Malcolm's head turned.

"Why? What's up?"

Malcolm quickly brought his sister up to speed with Gloria's concerns.

"Stewart Industries?" she asked. "What was Dad's dealing with them?"

"You know about them?"

"Yeah. They are this multibillion-dollar oil outfit with quite a reputation. I wonder what Dad's business was with them?"

"I don't know. It could be anything—or nothing."

"Hold on. Let me get Tyson on the line," she said.

Before he could object, the line clicked. A few seconds later, she returned while the new line rang.

"Hello."

"Tyson!" Shawnie greeted him. "It's me and Malcolm. You got a few minutes?"

"Sure. What's up?"

This time Shawnie related all that Malcolm had told her and they waited for his response.

"Hmm. That is odd," Tyson said. "I know I rely on my assistant for everything as well. I wouldn't dare book something without telling her."

"And Joe Dennis?"

"Well, to be frank, I always thought he was a little odd, myself. As far as the whole Stewart Industries angle, it could be anything. I wonder if there's any way to find out without raising any suspicion," Tyson said.

"Hmm. Maybe there is a way," Shawnie said almost absently.

"What do have in mind?" Malcolm asked.

"I don't know. Let me think about it. I'll get back with you."

Gloria sat up in bed and mopped her face. Her tears were giving her a migraine. She climbed out of bed, and her hand fell onto her satchel. She pulled out the cell phone bill again and her paranoia returned. "There is something going on," she muttered. "I can just feel it. But what?

"It wasn't an accident," she repeated. How had she forgotten about that? Sure, it could have been a prank, but grouped with the other strange events, she wasn't so sure. More than ever, she was beginning to regret not calling Drey St. John. If there was something to be found, surely he was the man to find it.

Gloria climbed out of bed, tossed some water onto her face and headed back out the door. She needed more information if she was going to talk to the private detective, and the only place to do that was back at the office.

When Gloria climbed into her car, night had descended. It was just as well, she decided. With the office closed and everyone gone, she would have more time and privacy to look—for what, she still wasn't sure. There had to be something. She was sure of it.

However, when Gloria entered the building, she wasn't alone.

Malcolm made his way over to Gloria's apartment building. Once he'd pulled into a parking space, he sucked in deep breaths to mount his courage. It had been a long time since he'd been in this position. Apologizing was never his forte—which had been the problem with his father. Had he apologized, they wouldn't have lost the past two years. He wasn't going to allow his pride to cost him Gloria's love.

He climbed out of his vehicle and marched up to the building, all the while rehearsing in his head what to say when she answered her door. It wasn't until he was standing before her door did he contemplate what he would do if she refused to let him in. Pulling himself together, he raised his hand and knocked.

He waited. After a lengthy silence, he tried again—his rap a little harder, but just as insistent. The third time, he hammered on the door. "Gloria, I know you're in there. Open up."

The door rattled.

"Gloria! Please let me in. I came to apologize."

At last, the sound of light footsteps padded toward the door. Malcolm straightened and gathered his composure, prepared to beg. When the door swung open, his eyes widened at the sight of a thinly built male, draped in a silk robe staring back at him.

"Oh." Malcolm stepped back and noticed the number on the door.

"Gloria doesn't live at this apartment," the man said in a breathy voice. "She lives next door." Pale green eyes roamed over Malcolm's body, while a hint of a smile curved his lips. "Lucky girl."

"Okay. Thank you. Sorry to disturb you," Malcolm said as he backed away.

"She's not home," the man said lazily.

Malcolm froze and turned back toward the neighbor.

"I saw her peel out of the parking lot like a bat out of hell about a half an hour ago."

"Do you know where she went?"

The man shrugged. "Knowing her, it had something to do with work. The girl is a workaholic."

"Thanks," Malcolm said, and rushed toward the elevators. His erratic driving bore a close resemblance to Gloria's as he raced across town. Knots twisted in his gut, making him jittery and anxious. He couldn't get to Gloria fast enough. When he arrived at his father's old building, he parked his

SUV next to Gloria's toy car. At least this time, he knew she was there.

Shutting off the engine, he sat for a moment, trying to rearrange the scrambled words inside his head, but after a few minutes he gave up. Malcolm remembered what he had said by his father's grave site. How he once believed he had the luxury of time.

He no longer held such delusions. If he wanted Gloria to love and to hold for the rest of his life, he had no more time to waste.

As he climbed out of his car and marched toward the building, he remembered the photograph of his parents' wedding day that his father had always kept on his desk. He remembered the certainty in each of their expressions and realized that was exactly how he felt about Gloria.

How he'd always felt about her.

Malcolm expected to have to buzz Gloria's office in order to get in, but he was surprised to find the door unlocked.

It was unlike Gloria to be so careless.

He stepped into the dark building, frowned when his hackles stood at attention. "Gloria?" he called out, thinking it was best not to scare her.

In answer, the office remained as quiet as a tomb while the air was charged with a strange energy. Something wasn't right.

"Gloria?" He crept toward her office, half expecting something to jump out of the shadows. His eyes strained to make out images in the dark. Though he'd been to the office countless times, he didn't have the lay of the place memorized, and he found himself bumping into a few desks and chairs the deeper he went.

At last, he rounded the corner to Gloria's office and frowned to see the door closed and no light peeking from under it. Surely she wasn't going to that great extreme to avoid him when her car was parked outside.

He knocked. "Gloria?"

No answer.

"C'mon, Gloria," he said, opening the door. "I know you're in here." He flipped on the light and froze when his eyes landed on Gloria sprawled across her office floor.

Chapter 21

"Gloria!" Malcolm ran to Gloria's side with his heart in his throat. Fear crawled up his spine. "Gloria." He gently turned her over in his arms and flinched. A gash on the left side of her temple was filled with blood and her face was utterly still. "Dear God. Don't you dare die on me," he commanded, shaking her body in a rising panic.

He couldn't lose her. Not like this. Not now.

He placed his fingers beneath her neck and searched for a pulse. When he found it beating faintly, steadily, he nearly collapsed with relief. Malcolm pulled Gloria's body close and wept.

* * *

Gloria's mind swam through inky blackness. When she caught the sound of a familiar voice calling out her name, she grew concerned by the sound of his heartbreaking sobs. He sounded so lost. She immediately felt the urge to comfort him. She struggled to break through her mind's spinning vortex until she could flutter her eyes open. She immediately regretted her actions when the light stabbed her eyes.

Moaning, she slammed her eyes shut again.

"Gloria?"

She finally recognized the familiar baritone, and it only deepened her confusion. "Malcolm?" She tried opening her eyes again, and this time, stared into eyes so filled with love that it overwhelmed her. "What are you doing here?" she asked in a scratchy voice. Bolts of pain shot through her head. She lifted her hand to find its source, only to pull it back wet and sticky.

"I'm bleeding," she said, stunned.

"I found you on the floor, passed out," Malcolm told her. "Do you remember what happened?"

Gloria tried to sit up, only for her head to threaten to explode.

"Don't move. Try to lie still and relax. I'm going to call the police."

"Police?" she questioned, as if she had never heard the word before.

Malcolm moved from her side and grabbed the telephone from the corner of her desk. He quickly punched in three numbers. "Yes. I'd like to report a break-in."

Gloria closed her eyes and tried to remember what had happened. Someone had been in her office. She tried to concentrate, ignoring the pain whenever she did so. She hadn't seen who it was. She just remembered pain shooting from the back of her head and then this sensation of falling, when she hit her head on the corner of the desk.

"The police and paramedics are on their way," Malcolm informed her, returning to her side. "How do you feel?"

"Like my head has been cracked open," she joked, but winced when she tried to laugh.

"Remember to try to remain still. Do you think you remember what happened now?"

Gloria slowly rolled her head from side to side. "Not really. I just remember coming into my office, but somebody was here."

"Who?" Malcolm's body tensed.

"I don't know. I didn't get a good look at him. He came out from behind me."

Malcolm glanced around; the office was trashed. "Someone was looking for something."

"Looking for what?"

"That's the million-dollar question. You're right about something shady and dangerous going on."

"You believe me?"

"It's kind of hard not to, given the circumstances." He smiled down at her and brushed away an errant curl. "Don't go to sleep on me. I need you to stay awake. You might have a concussion."

Gloria licked her lips and nodded. "What are you doing here?"

"I came to talk to you. I wanted to apologize for being an ass the past couple of weeks." His smile slowly ebbed away. "But when I saw you lying on this floor… Oh, Gloria. I'm so sorry I pushed you away. Can you ever forgive me? You're so right. I've been so scared to fall in love again. I found it so much easier to care for strangers than to invest my heart in something real."

"Malcolm—"

"You were right," he said, scared she was going to turn him down. "I was attracted to you the very first time I saw you—loved you from the first time we kissed. I came here tonight, prepared to beg you to take me back—to give me a second chance. I don't ever want to leave your side. Please tell me it's not too late."

Malcolm lost himself in the golden depths of her eyes and held his breath. What right did he have to hope that she would forgive him?

Gloria searched his gaze, as if to weigh whether he was telling her the truth, and then slowly a faint smile touched her lips and bloomed into something beautiful. She lifted a hand and cupped his cheek. "You were really going to beg?"

He smiled and turned his face to kiss the palm of her hand. "If that's what it took."

"Kiss me," she said.

Malcolm leaned forward and did as she commanded. It was meant to be a small peck because he didn't want to hurt her head, but one taste of her lips and he was lost. The next thing he knew he was overwhelmed by the very taste of her. "Oh, Gloria. I love you," he whispered, pulling away.

"Say it again," she said.

Malcolm found another inch to pull her closer. "I love you. I love you. I love you," he whispered against her ear. "Please say you'll marry me."

As if someone had waved a magic wand, Gloria's head cleared. "You want to marry me?"

"More than life itself."

Again, she searched his eyes and saw he meant it.

"Will you marry me?" he asked soberly.

Sheer joy filled Gloria as she threw her arms around Malcolm's neck and squeezed tight. "Yes. Yes. A thousand yeses." She paused; her smile faded.

"What's wrong?" he asked, suddenly fearful that she had changed her mind.

"Nothing. It's just that…don't you think we should at least go out on a real date? No political fund-raisers?"

Malcolm pulled her close. "Absolutely…but we're still getting married."

"Absolutely," she echoed.

Malcolm laughed before their lips found each other's.

A half an hour later, Malcolm and Gloria were surrounded by the police and paramedics. Both gave their accounts as to what had happened and read the disappointments on the officers' faces at the lack of details they were able to provide.

When Gloria felt woozy, the interviews ended and Malcolm accompanied her in the back of the ambulance to the hospital. Once there, Malcolm made sure that she received the best care available.

After the doctor completely checked Gloria over, he concluded that she had sustained a concussion and suggested that she stay for twenty-four-hours' surveillance.

Malcolm informed the staff that he'd be staying, as well. No sooner had the staff transferred Gloria to her room did the small Braddock clan join them. Concern and worry blanketed their faces.

"My dear, are you all right?" Evelyn asked, taking Gloria's hand and patting it lovingly. "We rushed over as soon as Malcolm called with the news."

Gloria smiled appreciatively. "Yes. I'm fine," she informed them. "It looks like my hard head came in handy."

Malcolm squeezed her hand lovingly, and then leaned over and pressed a kiss to her forehead.

Shocked, his family stared wide-eyed at them.

"Am I to take it that things have improved between you two?" Evelyn asked. A smile expanded across her face.

"More than improved," Malcolm said while his eyes remained locked onto Gloria's as he made an announcement. "We're engaged."

"What? So soon?" The women gasped in shock.

"Well," Malcolm said as he and Gloria beamed at each other, "we've known each other for a long time. When you know, you just know!" The women quite literally shoved Malcolm out of the way to give Gloria their congratulatory hugs and kisses.

To avoid making him feel left out, Tyson shoved a hand toward his older brother.

Malcolm took hold of it, but jerked Tyson close for a bear hug.

The jubilant smiles and hugs lasted for a long time. Evelyn insisted that the wedding be held at the family's estate and Malcolm and Gloria readily agreed. When asked for a date, the new couple glanced at each other.

"How about a Christmas wedding?" Evelyn suggested. "I think that would be lovely."

"Then Christmas it is."

"Does this mean that you're not going on your Malawi trip?" Shawnie asked.

Malcolm watched Gloria's face as he made his next announcement. "How can I go to Malawi when I have a campaign to run?"

On the heels of his question, the room fell silent for a second. The next second, his family erupted with a new wave of excitement.

A smile stretched across Gloria's face as tears brimmed her eyes.

Malcolm leaned forward and kissed her. This wasn't a small peck, but a kiss that bonded their souls together. When he pulled back, he lovingly wiped her tears from her face.

"You don't have to do this for me," she whispered.

"It's not just for you, but for myself, my father and, more important, for the causes I truly believe in."

"When did you make this decision?" she asked.

"Just now." He kissed the tip of her nose. "It took

me a while to figure out but I think it's my calling. Are you happy?"

"Only if this is something you truly want to do. I don't want you to think I want you to be like your father."

Malcolm's smile grew. "You know, I'm thinking that being like my father isn't such a bad thing, after all." Their lips melted together once more.

While lost in their own private world, neither of them heard his family as they exited the room, giving them their privacy.

As the night grew late, Malcolm remained by Gloria's side. So much so that he risked the staff's wrath by climbing into the narrow bed with her.

"Did I ever tell you how much I love spooning with you?" he whispered.

"Malcolm, we're in a hospital."

"I know. Kind of exciting, huh?" He nibbled on her earlobe and slid his hand down her back. "I love the easy access provided by these hospital gowns, too."

"Malcolm." She giggled a weak warning. "If you don't behave they're going to toss you out of here."

"Not if we keep quiet, Mrs. Braddock—like we did at my mother's place."

"I'm not Mrs. Braddock yet."

"Let's pretend that you are." He snuggled her

neck and dipped his hand between her legs.
Malcolm only wanted to tease her, but once they got
started, there was no turning back.

Gloria, still giggling, couldn't believe what they
were about to do until they were doing it. Her legs
opened to him easily while her eyes closed lazily
when he slid into her and began moving.

Malcolm buried his face into her hair and breathed
deeply while pleasure raced down her spine. Her
body was inflamed by his every stroke. She curled
toward him, seeking her body's ultimate release.

Their bodies rocked together in silent harmony.
Gloria panted and then bit into her pillow in order not
to cry out, while one hand gripped the bed's railing.

Malcolm's eyes rolled to the back of his head
when he felt her tightening around him, gripping
him as if she'd never let him go.

Their orgasms blasted through them simultaneously, leaving them shuddering and quaking in
ecstasy.

Spent, Malcolm drizzled kisses on the back of
her neck, while from the bottom of his heart he confessed, "I love you, Gloria. Now and forever."

"Is that your first campaign promise?"

"No. This is my life's promise."

Epilogue

The next morning, Malcolm and Gloria waited for the doctor to okay her release from the hospital. They were surprised by a sudden stream of visitors. First Senator Cayman strolled into the room and Malcolm and Gloria blinked in surprise.

"Senator," Gloria said, smiling. "What are you doing here?"

He smiled awkwardly as he approached. "I heard the news. I came right over. Are you all right?"

"Yes. It's no more than a bump on the head," she admitted sheepishly.

Malcolm frowned. "How did you hear about what happened?"

"News travels fast in the law enforcement community."

As if to confirm his statement, suddenly there was another knock on the door.

Malcolm blinked at the familiar face, struggling to place it.

"Mr. St. John." Gloria exclaimed.

"Hello, Gloria," he greeted her with a nod, first to her and then to Malcolm and the senator. "I heard about the break-in. I came to see if you were all right."

"Thanks, but I'm fine." Gloria turned toward Malcolm. "This is Drey St. John, a private investigator and a good friend of your father's."

Malcolm perked up at that. "A private investigator? Didn't I see you at my father's funeral?"

"Yes. I came and paid my respects. Your father was a good friend." He extended his hand and Malcolm accepted. He liked the man immediately.

"I hear the police don't have any leads. I'm here to offer my services. I can poke around if you like."

Malcolm grabbed hold of Gloria's hand, and then said, "Thanks, but for the moment, we've decided to let the police look into it."

Drey nodded. "I completely understand. But, hey, if you ever change your mind, I'm available."

"We'll keep that in mind," Malcolm said, and meant it.

Drey tossed a smile at Gloria and then nodded to the two men before he headed out of the room.

On his way out, Judge Hanlon strolled in. He also nodded his greeting to everyone in the room. "I came as soon as I heard. Is everything all right?"

"Yes, yes. I'm starting to feel like a little celebrity," Gloria said. "I'm fine, really."

"Any idea what they were looking for?"

While Gloria went on to fill the senator and the judge in on what had happened last night, Malcolm stepped out into the hallway to search for the doctor. Instead, he saw his brother strolling toward him.

"How's it going?" Tyson asked.

"Good. Good. Just waiting around for the doctor to come and release her." He lifted his brows. "So what are you doing here—come to help me take her home or something?"

"Not exactly."

Malcolm frowned. "How come I don't like the sound of that?"

"Because you're probably not going to like what I have to tell you."

"All right." Malcolm crossed his arms. "What is it?"

"Well, it seems our sister has taken it into her

head to become Nancy Drew and do some investigating of her own."

"I'm not following you."

"She's starting a new job...with Stewart Industries."

DON'T MISS
THIS SEXY NEW SERIES
FROM KIMANI ROMANCE!

THE BRADDOCKS

SECRET SON

*Power, passion and politics
are all in the family.*

HER LOVER'S LEGACY by Adrianne Byrd
August 2008

SEX AND THE SINGLE BRADDOCK
by Robyn Amos
September 2008

SECOND CHANCE, BABY by A.C. Arthur
October 2008

THE OBJECT OF HIS PROTECTION
by Brenda Jackson
November 2008

www.kimanipress.com

KPBSS0808

She went looking for treasure…
and rediscovered temptation!

MEET PHOENIX

Book #2 in Romance on the Run

National Bestselling Author

MARCIA KING-GAMBLE

Art expert Phoenix Sutherland vows to remain
professional when her sexy ex-husband joins her
expedition to recover a priceless statue. But it's not
long before the thrill of danger rekindles sparks
of desire neither can resist.

TOP SECRET

ROMANCE ON THE RUN

Available the first week of August wherever books are sold.

KIMANI™
ROMANCE

www.kimanipress.com

KPMKG0770808

Just one look was all it took....

always a
KNIGHT

Book #3 in The Knight Family trilogy

Bestselling Author
WAYNE JORDAN

Aspiring songstress Tori Matthews stirs such
passion in Russell Knight, she's just the girl to change
his playboy ways. But as things begin to heat up
between them, Tori is forced to choose between their
growing passion and a shot at stardom.

"Jordan weaves an unbelievably romantic story
with enough twists and turns to keep any reader
enthralled until the very end."
—*Romantic Times BOOKreviews*
on ONE GENTLE KNIGHT

Available the first week of August wherever books are sold.

KIMANI™
ROMANCE

www.kimanipress.com   KPWJ0780808

How she loved to hate that man!

RIVAL'S *Desire*

Favorite author

ALTONYA WASHINGTON

Enemies since childhood, Vivian and Caesar are caught
in their matchmaking grandmothers' scheme to bring
them together. The problem for Caesar is that Vivian
knows him too well. But now he wants to know her—
every inch of her—for a lifetime.

Available the first week of August wherever books are sold.

KIMANI™
ROMANCE

www.kimanipress.com

KPAW0790808

"Donna Hill has written another tear-your-heart-out but jump-for-joy-in-the-end sizzler that will keep the reader coming back for more."
—*Romantic Times BOOKreviews*
on CHANCES ARE

ESSENCE BESTSELLING AUTHOR

DONNA HILL

Chances Are

Knowing from personal experience the hardships faced by unwed mothers, Dionne Williams established a successful home for teenage mothers and their babies. But when TV producer Garrett Lawrence does a story on the center, Dionne battles conflicting emotions about her overpowering attraction to a man so cynical about unwed mothers.

Available the first week of August, wherever books are sold.

ARABESQUE®
www.kimanipress.com

KPDHI070808

When lightning strikes,
there's no holding back...

NATIONAL BESTSELLING AUTHOR

ROCHELLE ALERS

Taken by Storm

Book #3 of The Whitfield Brides trilogy

When Marshal Raphael Madison becomes
Simone Whitfield's live-in bodyguard during a
high-profile trial, Simone finds his presence stirs up a
storm of longing. Soon their electrifying closeness leads
to an endless night of uncontrollable passion. But will the
morning after bring regrets…or promises of forever?

Meet the Whitfields of New York—experts at coordinating
other people's weddings, but not so great at arranging
their own love lives.

Available the first week of August, wherever books are sold.

ARABESQUE®

www.kimanipress.com

KPRAI100808

Dark, rich and delicious…how could she resist?

NATIONAL BESTSELLING AUTHOR

ROCHELLE ALERS

The Sweetest Temptation

Book #2 of The Whitfield Brides trilogy

Faith Whitfield's been too busy satisfying the sweet tooth of others
to lament her own love life. But when Ethan McMillan comes
to her rescue, he finds himself falling for the luscious pastry
chef…and soon their passions heat to the boiling point!

Meet the Whitfields of New York—experts at
coordinating other people's weddings, but not so great
at arranging their own love lives.

Available the first week of July wherever books are sold.

ARABESQUE®

www.kimanipress.com   KPRA1020708

011 +353 3861937057

NATIONAL BESTSELLING AUTHOR

ROCHELLE ALERS

invites you to meet the Whitfields of New York....

Tessa, Faith and Simone Whitfield know all about coordinating
other people's weddings, and not so much about arranging
their own love lives. But in the space of one unforgettable year,
all three will meet intriguing men who just might bring them their
very own happily ever after....

Long Time Coming

June 2008

The Sweetest Temptation

July 2008

Taken by Storm

August 2008

ARABESQUE®

www.kimanipress.com

KPALERSTRIL08